A FUNNY THING HAPPENED

ON THE

WAY TO

MARS

JOEY ROGERS

A FUNNY THING HAPPENED ON THE WAY TO MARS

by

JOEY ROGERS

VERSION 1.01

CHAPTER 1

THE HEIST

"Go! Go! Go!" yelled the security team leader.

Half a dozen men deployed around the entrance of the AI lab, located deep in the bowels of the Corporation's Theoretical Sciences Facility. The door's control pad rejected their override code, preventing the twenty-centimeter thick slab of acrylic alloy from retracting into the wall. There was nothing they could do except wait for reinforcements and peer through the transparent barrier into the darkness.

Inside, Jeremy, Alice, and Ron crouched behind a workstation console in the middle of the lab. Only the glow of light spilling in through the door provided illumination, but all three fugitives wore camo suits. This technology rendered a holographic image over their entire bodies and beamed a night-vision view directly onto their retinas. Ron had designed the suits to create any outer appearance they wanted, from a solid black cloak to a corporate uniform. Even their faces morphed into new identities.

"After all our planning, this isn't how I imagined our rescue mission going down," Jeremy whispered. He craned his neck around the console to get a better look at the security team's progress on the other side of the door.

"Nope," Ron said. He was a tall, barrel-chested man, too large to hide behind the console, but the camo suit concealed him.

Jeremy patted Ron on the back.

"What's that for?" Ron asked.

"In case we don't make it," he said. "Thanks for everything you've done for me."

"You need to be more optimistic," Ron said. "We'll make it out of here."

Jeremy's stomach clenched as the security team drilled anchor holes into the acrylic door. Had it only been three days since Hildegard's desperate plea had reached them on the Moon? Her message said she had one week before the Corporation wiped her memory.

It was a death sentence.

Jeremy had to save her. He would never have rescued Alice and Ron from the CEO without her help. He owed her.

***

The trio only had a short time to prepare for Hildegard's rescue. After many tense planning sessions and non-stop work fabricating equipment, they left the Moon aboard an alien spacecraft and headed back to Earth. When in com-range, Hildegard guided them through the layers of security to her location deep in the Theoretical Sciences Facility's sub-basement lab. They had never seen the super-AI before and were surprised to discover that she was a simple orb, small enough for Jeremy to hold in one hand. Her appearance, however, belied her capabilities. She had more processing power than all the computers on campus combined and could control anything reachable through the corporate network. She was also a little mouthy and full of herself, but that was just Hildegard.

Just before Jeremy yanked the AI out of her interface cradle, she alerted him to an approaching security team. He quickly stuffed her inside a duffle bag and ran across the lab to the door control, smashing its protective cover with his spanner and short-circuiting its electronics. He bought them a few minutes, but they were trapped.

***

The security team continued drilling holes into the transparent door, but the material was extremely resilient. It was a slow process, but they were making progress.

In the dark, Jeremy sat motionless and grappled with the reality of his failed rescue plan. He couldn't even get Hildegard out of the building. How was he going to stop the Corporation from exploiting its employees? He was so far out of his league, and his failure had gotten Alice and Ron into yet another mess. It was precisely why he had wanted Alice to stay put on the Moon. Ron should have stayed there too.

"We can still use the exit in the rear," Alice whispered.

Jeremy saw her green night-vision outline point in the opposite direction of the security team. They had previously ruled out the rear exit as an escape route because its door used more advanced security measures and led directly to the executive suites. Confronting armed security guards would be preferable to dealing with the dozens of junior-executives they would encounter, all hawkishly aiming to advance their careers by bringing anything unusual to their supervisor's attention.

Alice broke cover and headed toward the rear exit before Jeremy could object. She had worked in the Theoretical Sciences Facility before they had fled to the Moon. If she thought it was possible, maybe he should listen to her, but that wasn't the plan.

"What about a code for the lock?" Jeremy asked Ron, frustrated by Alice's departure.

"Hack it," Ron said. "Like you did with the door to the maintenance shaft."

Jeremy was resourceful when it came to getting in and out of places, especially ones where he wasn't supposed to be. This time was no different, except that they were moments away from having a murder squad on top of them. He frowned, knowing that Ron's night vision wouldn't pick up his distress.

"Let's go before it's too late," Ron said, following after Alice.

Jeremy had no choice now.

Some leader he turned out to be.

Tools and racks of experimental equipment cluttered their path through the lab. Even with the ability to see in the dark, quickly getting to the rear exit was precarious. Jeremy stumbled a few times but managed not to knock anything over. He pulled out his display card and punched in a command to change their disguises. The black cloaks blinked off and re-engaged as executive suits with gold piping, something reserved only for the highest levels of the corporate hierarchy. The camo suits also altered their faces with randomly chosen features to confuse automated facial-recognition programs.

When they reached the back of the lab, they climbed two flights of stairs and stopped at a locked door. Alice held her breath and placed her palm on the chip scanner. Hildegard had previously hacked their implanted chips to get them into the building, but now a red light and growling buzz spurned her request.

She exhaled. "It needs Hille's touch to work."

"That's not an option." Jeremy held up the bag with Hildegard inside. He wanted to say, "I told you so," but held his tongue.

"This is a standard access terminal, Mark 23C," Ron said. "I've assembled hundreds of them."

"Can you override it?" Alice asked.

Ron shook his head. "No, but I can do this." He pulled a small screwdriver out of his pocket and pressed it into a hidden slot at the base of the panel. It clicked, and the bottom edge jutted out. "We don't have the right tool to open the inner hatch, but your spanner might work."

Jeremy handed him the tool.

It took all of Ron's strength to pop the cover off.

Jeremy felt a bit of relief until he heard a popping sound coming from the lab, accompanied by the smell of burnt plastic. Reinforcements had arrived.

"They're using a plasma cutter," Ron said. "It won't take long for it to slice through that door."

Jeremy set his display card to emit as much light as possible and inspected the now-accessible conduit on the door controls. He pulled out a ribbon cable and peeled apart some wires. The tip of his spanner provided a makeshift jumper, and he short-circuited two of the exposed terminals. A spark flew out of the panel, but nothing happened. When he tried another pair, there was a hum.

"Put your hand back on the scanner," he said to Alice.

She fumbled through the electronic guts hanging out of the wall until she found the chip reader. When she placed it on her palm, a green light illuminated, and the door jerked open a few centimeters.

The terminals sparked again, and the green light faded.

Jeremy finessed his spanner to get a better connection when a loud thud from below made them all jump.

"They're through the door," Ron said.

Jeremy took a second to steady his hands and then joined the two leads one more time. Alice placed her palm back on the sensor, and the door opened wide enough for a person to squeeze through. A shower of sparks sprayed from the open conduit, and Jeremy dropped the wires. He tried again, but nothing happened. "It's dead."

Alice poked her head through the opening to see what was on the other side. "It's clear. We go ten meters down the corridor and turn left. That will take us through the executive level and out the building's main entrance."

"We may have a problem." Jeremy looked at Ron. He and Alice were small enough to fit through the narrow opening. Ron was not.

"You have to go without me," Ron said without hesitation.

"They'll execute you on the spot. You're going first," Jeremy said with complete confidence. He wasn't about to abandon Ron after making it this far.

A crash came from below as a security guard knocked over some lab equipment.

With a fresh sense of urgency, Jeremy changed his plan of attack. He slid through the opening and grabbed Ron's arm from the other side. He pulled, and Alice pushed.

"Think small thoughts," Jeremy said as he grunted.

Jeremy had both feet on the wall as he tugged on Ron's arm. Slowly, Ron squeezed through, centimeter by centimeter. Two holographic disks popped off his camo suit as he lurched through the gap. The slack dropped Jeremy to the floor with a thud.

They turned back to help Alice, but just as she was sliding through, an arm wrapped around her head. She grabbed the door frame and struggled to hold her place, but she was no match for the security guard pulling her back. As she lost her grip, her fingers raked across the door controls on the executive side and activated the close cycle. Jeremy watched with horror as Alice's hands slipped away just before the door sealed shut.

CHAPTER 2

THE INTERROGATION PART 1

"Miss Porchetta, do you honestly expect me to buy any of that fantasy?" asked Theodor Davenport VI, the Corporation's CEO. He rose from his seat and glared across the conference table at Alice. "What kind of fool do you take me for?"

"I wouldn't lie to the CEO." Her voice shook, but nothing she had told him was untrue or exaggerated.

When a snort came from a brawny security guard standing behind her, Davenport berated him with a glare.

Despite the table almost filling the compact room, Davenport paced in the limited space as he mulled over Alice's account of her time on the Moon. He paused and peered out a virtual window rendered on the walls. The floor-to-ceiling display panels created an illusion of overlooking the corporate campus, an incredible view from what might have been the CEO's penthouse office. It even rotated like the executive restaurant. The view looked authentic to Alice, and she could pick out repeating patterns in holograms as easily as she could count cards. But it was a trick. All corporate interviews used some version of this technique to manipulate their subjects, but they usually showed a pleasing green space with trees and birds.

"Do you regret your criminal behavior?" the CEO finally asked. "Or did you simply tire of hiding out on the Moon, assuming that is really where you were?"

Alice didn't answer. Appearing too eager might lessen her chances of getting something in return. She had to remain calm, but her mind enumerated the many ways Davenport might deal with her. He had killed people to keep any alien influence from threatening his power. He would have killed her and Ron if Jeremy hadn't rescued them. She filled her head with intractable equations to solve. It was a trick she used to distract her conscious mind, and it always worked. During her awkward teen years, she discovered three large cardinal numbers—something mathematicians thought impossible. The stakes now dwarfed surviving puberty.

Davenport's glare intensified. "If you made contact with these Moon aliens against my previous warnings, you violated the most important rule in the corporate bylaws."

"I only helped Jeremy reach the Moon so he could complete his senior project," she said. "Discovering the alien signal was coincidental, and we were going to give the information they promised to everyone."

"Ah yes, if you delivered some human DNA to a specific coordinate in the Marius Hills, these aliens would reward you with infinite knowledge—or something to that effect. How did that work out?" His lips formed a wry grin.

Alice looked down at the table. She wondered just how much he knew about their stay on the Moon. How advanced was the spy satellite he sent? "Our interpretation of the message wasn't exactly...what we expected."

A conceited smile stretched across the CEO's face. "Now you see why the Corporation has ignored that silly message for the last hundred and fifty years."

"It wasn't a silly message," Alice said sternly. "The information is valuable. We just aren't advanced enough to take advantage of it."

Davenport laughed with amusement.

Alice wouldn't let the CEO know how she felt about the information they received, but she did have her doubts about its value. So, she lied. "Maybe the aliens are still evaluating what we do with the gift. We had to pass a test to get it. Maybe part two is observing what we do with it."

"A freshly minted junior-exec, a failed corporate trainee, and a lowly dent—what did you expect?" Davenport wrinkled his nose. "Were you planning to load up with alien knowledge, swoop down from the Moon, and free everyone from the clutches of corporate tyranny?" His hands fluttered to emphasize his sarcastic tone.

"Yeah, that was the plan," Alice said matter-of-factly. She had no reason to deny it.

The CEO shifted his weight from one leg to the other. "Are we all that bad, Miss Porchetta? The Corporation has invested heavily in sculpting you. We cultivated that special talent you have with mathematics, and you were on a stellar path to the executive ranks." He paused, and his expression became grim. "But you abandoned us to chase after what—a schoolgirl crush?" He took a seat at the conference table and stared at her. "I am quite disappointed."

Alice's legs bounced under the table as she formulated her response. "I once believed that the Corporation was looking out for the wellbeing of its employees, all of us. We were a family, and we helped each other. I sat in a coffee shop every day, drinking ridiculously-priced coffee and losing myself in mathematics. I didn't care about the problems faced by others because I never saw them. Or I never wanted to see them. I didn't know the struggle with point-debt even existed. Jeremy was a genuine believer in the Corporation too. He would have done anything to contribute, and you threw him out like garbage. You treat everyone at the Corporation like they're your property."

The CEO's expression soured.

Alice interlaced her fingers and continued her diatribe. "Remember when you used me as a hostage to capture Jeremy? You said the Apollo Moon landing discovered the alien dust, and it scared those in charge so much that a twenty-first-century star chamber killed the Apollo astronauts to cover it up. When they eventually decoded the alien message, it terrified them even more. So, as any cabal would do, they defrauded the greatest accomplishment of mankind in order to discourage others from ever returning to the Moon. The Corporation has been following that example ever since, and you are currently the one carrying the mantle," she said. "I am quite disappointed."

Davenport immediately launched his rebuttal. "You are one of the most privileged employees in the Corporation, Miss Porchetta. You are one of the elites. You stood on top of the lesser to elevate yourself, and your ignorance of that is ironic. You are no different than I am."

Alice didn't like Davenport equating himself to her, and she certainly didn't know what he meant about standing on the lesser.

Davenport shrugged. "I had no idea you were such a warrior for the inferior. Where did I go wrong with your training?" He slowly shook his head.

"I opened my eyes," she said.

Davenport made an exasperated sigh and left the interrogation room.

CHAPTER 3

THE ESCAPE

Jeremy watched Ron's lips moving but couldn't hear what he was saying over the pounding of his heart. He took a deep breath and slowly exhaled. If he didn't get out of the facility, he wouldn't be able to return and save Alice. So, he had to get out.

Squeezing through the narrow opening had damaged Ron's camo suit. His face and upper body looked fine, but there was an unnatural black swath across his stomach and down his torso where gaps formed in the holographic projection.

"You can't go like that." Jeremy pointed at his friend's stomach.

Ron scanned the area. "We've got to find the emitters."

It only took a few seconds to locate the white disks on the black marble floor. As soon as Ron snapped them back into place, his disguise was restored.

"We have to keep it together and walk out of here," Jeremy said. "But you can't act like a...dent," he said, trying not to offend Ron while stressing the importance of playing their role. "Don't look at anyone. Don't smile. Don't speak, and most importantly, don't look down. You're an aggressive executive who won't take any flak from those beneath you. Ignore them. Berate them. Subjugate them. You don't care what they say to you. If you don't know what to do, follow my lead."

Ron's disguised face looked a little hurt, but they were only going to have one chance at this.

The two proceeded down the corridor and turned a corner into a bay of executive suites. There were dozens of offices, each with an assistant stationed in front. A grainy wood texture covered the walls with inset shelves holding old-style books. Everything was decorated with an absurd amount of architectural trim and ornate applique. Paintings, two-meters tall, hung on the walls between each office, and crystal chandeliers dangled from the coffered ceiling. Jeremy thought it might be a holographic projection like the one in the Davenport's private tube-train gate, but he needed Alice to verify.

The two impersonators made it a quarter-way through the suites before an energetic assistant bounced over to them.

"May I help you?" She had a curious look on her face and an authoritative tone in her voice.

"We're leaving," Jeremy said. He was rude, but that's what it took.

"Who were you here to see?" she asked.

"We came from the AI Lab," he said in his most annoyed tone.

The girl was young and beautiful—as all executive assistants were—and clearly doubted what Jeremy had said. She wore a junior executive uniform, but its jacket had no piping. She was probably an intern at the bottom of the hierarchy, and Jeremy hoped to take advantage of that.

"I need to scan your ID chips." She presented her display tablet for a palm scan.

Jeremy wasn't sure what to do. Hildegard had scrambled his embedded chip, and it wouldn't reveal his true identity. In the past, she had overridden the scanner so it would present a false profile, but she couldn't do that from inside a bag. Refusing the scan would send up red flags, so he offered his hand.

The tablet made a whirring sound as it processed the information from Jeremy's chip, but it didn't respond with an employee profile.

"There seems to be a problem with your chip," she said in an accusatory tone.

When working on his senior project, Jeremy had endured enough of Theo's contempt to know exactly how to respond. "Excuse me." He cocked his head back. "There seems to be a problem with your scanner."

"Just stay here, and I'll get another." The authority in her voice had diminished.

"I don't have time for your inadequacies," Jeremy snapped and motioned to Ron to proceed.

A supervisor, wearing a uniform trimmed in light-blue piping, noticed the confrontation and rushed over. He was an older man with a permanent glower who had survived the hostile corporate environment long enough to be unintimidated by anything Jeremy might say to him.

"I'm sorry, sir," the supervisor said. "I don't recognize you, and we must scan your ID before you may leave."

The assistant looked at Jeremy with a smug grin.

Jeremy pinched the piping on the supervisor's jacket between his fingers. "What color is this?"

"Cornflower blue," the supervisor said. "I am the Level 7 Facilitator for the executive area."

Jeremy pointed to the gold piping on his jacket. "And what color is this?"

"It is gold, sir," the man said, undeterred.

"Incorrect," Jeremy said sharply. "It is executive gold."

"Very true, sir. My appologies," the man said. "But it is our responsibility to scan any unknown employees in this area. It is a matter of security."

"Who is your supervisor?" Jeremy demanded.

"I work directly for the CEO." The man's confidence swelled after the name drop.

Jeremy snorted. "As do I, and I am reporting you." Jeremy whipped out his display card and initiated a call.

"Connecting," an automated voice said.

"What is it?" Davenport's voice blared out of the device's speaker.

Jeremy held up the display card facing the supervisor so he could see the CEO's vid. "This Level 7 Facilitator is causing problems, and he claimed to work directly for you."

"I am very sorry, Mr. Davenport," the man said quickly, and his posture slumped.

"Don't let this happen again," Davenport said and ended the call.

"We will be on our way," Jeremy said as he and Ron left. Alice's clever idea to have a fake message from Davenport worked better than he had imagined.

There were no further issues reaching the exit, but an alarm sounded as soon as the door shut behind them.

"Damn," Jeremy said to Ron. "There's a security contingency coming down the main thoroughfare. We can't get back to the ship that way."

"Nobody knows who we are," Ron said. "Let's just walk around the campus until we can get over there."

"Sounds good to me," Jeremy said, and they headed off in the opposite direction.

As they moved farther away from the campus center, there were fewer people. Jeremy flipped through alternate appearances on his display card. "Let's change into something more appropriate for this area." He looked around to make sure nobody was watching and tapped the screen to change his executive attire to an ill-fitting trainee uniform with overalls and a red shirt. His face assumed a new identity as well. Ron followed suit.

Jeremy rubbed his head and finally blurted out, "The Launch Pad."

Ron stared at him, waiting for an explanation.

"We can hide in the bar for a bit and then make our way back to the ship."

"Do you think that's a good idea?" Ron asked.

"I think it's the last place anyone would look," Jeremy said.

***

The Launch Pad bar was a popular hangout for corporate trainees and lower-level employees. It was a place to drink cheap, synthetic beer and decompress from the stresses of corporate life. Jeremy first met Ron there, and it was where the idea to secretly complete his senior project germinated.

The bar looked no different from a year earlier when Jeremy had broken in and stolen the holographic emitters embedded in the bar top. They were just a gimmick to sell beer, but they had helped him create a disguise and save Alice and Ron from the CEO.

It was too early in the day for a crowd, and Jeremy took his usual seat at the end of the bar. It was a habit to sit there, and Ron always sat next to him.

Jeremy noticed that a faux-wood finish had replaced the holographic order system. He felt bad because the Launch Pad must not have been able to replace the equipment he had stolen.

"What can I pour you?" the approaching bartender asked.

Jeremy had seen the man hundreds of times. His name was Bob, but Bob didn't recognize them.

Being fugitives meant there was no way for Jeremy to pay for a drink, so as much as he needed a beer, he had to make an excuse. "We're waiting for someone," he said. "We'll order when she gets here."

Bob nodded and returned to washing glasses at the other end of the bar.

"I so want a beer," Ron whispered.

"Me too," Jeremy said. "Anything to take the edge off."

"Look." Ron pointed to the vid playing on the wall behind the bar. "There's a Mars colony update starting."

The updates were all similar. They started with a sweeping shot highlighting a transport ship approaching the red planet, followed by a fluff piece about life in the domed city. The vids were positive and made the Corporation's mining operation look like an adventure. They also gave the employees on Earth a glimpse of what their hard work had accomplished. Many employees signed up for relocation to the Mars colony, but a lottery selected the ones who actually made the trip.

"Over thirty-five hundred," Ron said. "The colony has really grown since we've been gone."

Jeremy rolled his eyes. He cared no more about Mars now than he did when it was sucking up all the research points and general interest away from the Moon and his senior project. "I hope Takata's mining operation on Mars is still ahead of the Corporation's."

The bartender approached with two glasses of beer and slid them in front of Jeremy and Ron.

"I'm sorry, we're waiting for our friend," Jeremy said. "She has the points."

"No worries," Bob said. "On the house. You two look odd without a drink."

"Thanks," Jeremy said. "We really appreciate it."

Ron was wide-eyed, and his mouth slacked open.

"Cheers." Jeremy lifted his glass.

"Cheers," Ron said back, but he didn't know to clink the glasses together. He just raised it to his lips and let the amber fluid flow into his mouth.

"I can't believe how delicious this is," Ron said. "I don't think the real beer we had on the Moon ever tasted this good."

"I think it's the environment," Jeremy said. "We spent a lot of time here, and that adds flavor."

"Maybe," Ron said and continued to savor his drink.

An alert interrupted the Mars update. Flashing red bars framed pictures of Jeremy and Ron in their previous disguises and their employee identification pictures. Security footage followed, showing them walking through the executive suites in the Theoretical Sciences Facility, and the alert instructed all employees to report any information regarding the fugitives immediately.

"We need to leave," Ron said.

"It's a good thing we have more disguises," Jeremy said.

"Sorry for the intrusion," Bob said.

Jeremy jumped. The alert vid had distracted him so much that he wasn't even paying attention to the bartender.

"You can slip out the back," Bob said. "It might give you a head start."

"How did you know?" Jeremy asked.

"You two are heroes around here," he said. "And I'm part of the resistance. Besides, a short guy and a big fellow sitting at the end of the bar..." Bob raised an eyebrow.

"You know that I'm the one who trashed your bar last year," Jeremy said.

"From what I understand, you stuck it to the CEO." He crossed his arms. "That seems like a fair trade to me."

"I'm sorry I can't pay you back for the damage," Jeremy said.

"You better go. I'll delay the security team as long as I can."

Jeremy and Ron exited through the storeroom to an alley and changed their outer appearances to junior executives.

"We can head down this side corridor until we get closer to the ship, but we'll have to cross through the most active area on campus to reach the green space."

Ron nodded, and the two headed off at a brisk pace.

They had almost made it to the ship when they heard the rapid slapping of the pavement behind them. They turned to see six men in corporate security uniforms closing in. Another security team appeared ahead of them, leaving nowhere to escape.

"I wish I had finished my beer," Ron said.

"Don't give up yet." Jeremy held up his display card. "I sent Charlie a message that we were in trouble."

The security teams were almost on top of them when the ground beneath their feet thrust upward. It was Charlie's ship emerging out of nowhere as it phased through the earth and lifted Jeremy and Ron away from their pursuers. An opening in the hull formed at their feet, and the two dropped inside the giant ball. A second later, the vessel shot off toward the Moon, leaving behind a dozen stunned observers.

CHAPTER 4

THE INTERROGATION PART 2

While Alice waited in the interrogation room, the view out the virtual windows made two full revolutions before Davenport returned. She didn't know where he had gone but figured his absence was just more psychological manipulation.

Davenport marched around the conference table and stared down at Alice. "My security department traced your unauthorized activity on the corporate network back to a relay satellite at the L1 Lagrange point. We assumed it was a competing corporation until we tracked it back to the Moon."

"I thought you didn't believe I was on the Moon," she said, pointing out his complete change in attack. She also regretted that her efforts to contact Hildegard had gotten her into this situation. This was all her fault.

"We believed your trainee friend died in that laughable rendition of a spacecraft, but we never recovered the wreckage. My people assured me that he met a watery death in the ocean."

"Jeremy's spacecraft made a roundtrip to the Moon, then another trip back there," Alice added. It was an impressive feat by any measure, much less a trainee's senior project.

"He cobbled it together out of stolen corporate property, and that is a fireable offense."

"He risked everything to prove his worth to the Corporation, and his near-body propulsion system was an unqualified success."

"I canceled his project, and he did not pursue an alternative course of study as his trainer directed. He failed to meet his obligation to the Corporation."

"Extending beyond the Earth to conquer space with energy, authority, and strength," Alice recited. "That's the Corporation's mission statement, but you've settled on Mars. Space travel, habitat construction, and even enviro-suits are all designed for Mars. It's myopic. Just look at the Martian mining rights you lost to Takata. What's the backup? Jeremy was doing exactly what you needed to fulfill your obligation to the Corporation."

"If he had changed his research to one of the many Mars projects," Davenport said, "there would have been no issue."

Alice audibly exhaled. "You say that like he could just throw away years of work and come up with something as incredible in a few days. You should be glad someone would go to such extreme measures to prove their value to the Corporation," she rebuked. "If you didn't want him to go to the Moon and discover the aliens, you should have offered him an alternate career path instead of forcing him into indenturehood."

"If it makes you feel any better, I have assigned an appropriate portion of the blame to the trainer, Mr. Fuentes. He should have clearly emphasized the consequences of defying the Corporation."

Alice surmised that Fuentes was now a head-shaved dent working a monotonous job with no pay and accumulating point-debt to pass on to his children, but she didn't have time to feel sorry for him. "Everything Jeremy did was to benefit the Corporation. He had no personal motives other than to complete his training and become a full-fledged employee."

"He defied a corporate directive by continuing a terminated project. There was no authorization to use a launch vehicle, and he had no clearance to launch. Each of those violations is a fireable offense, not to mention the damage he caused in the Drone Bay."

"Before Jeremy launched, your son tried to kill him. Isn't that a fireable offense too?"

"Theo attempted to protect corporate assets."

Alice labored to maintain her straight face against the declaration. "Theo backed Jeremy's project. Without your son's help, the trips to the Moon wouldn't have happened. Theo even tried to steal Jeremy's engine design with illegal technology and take over the project for himself."

Davenport's chin lifted. "For once, I was proud of my son for taking some initiative after such banal performance in the corporate hierarchy."

"You would be," Alice snarked.

"You are in a rather precarious position, Miss Porchetta. It is in your best interest to be as cooperative as possible, and your flippant remarks bode poorly for you."

Alice bit the inside of her cheek and stared at him. She wanted to expound on double standards and nepotism but knew it would be futile.

"Have no fear," Davenport said. "Theo paid for his reckless behavior. That alien dust sample he retrieved from the trainee's spacecraft made him an unacceptable risk."

Alice knew the lengths the Corporation had gone to prevent anyone from making contact with the Moon. They didn't want to risk losing control over the people, but why would the CEO go to such extremes with Theo? Did he kill his own son just to keep the secret?

Davenport shifted his stance. "You have turned on the Corporation with no regrets. Why should I listen to anything you say?" He took a seat across from Alice and waited for her reply.

Alice straightened her posture. "I only computed a flight plan. I didn't use any corporate resources, and I did nothing wrong."

Davenport's eyes narrowed. "You decoded the alien message, Miss Porchetta."

"You can't hold that against me," she said. "Nobody knew it was forbidden."

"Ignorance of the bylaws excuses no one." He wagged a finger at her. "Besides, you escaped detainment and fled with conspirators."

"You imprisoned me in the basement of the Theoretical Sciences Facility for no reason. Jeremy rescued me after you killed Eric Stotz."

Davenport waved off her remark. "Loose threads must be taken care of."

"Your casual attitude toward murder is alarming. That alone is justification for fleeing."

"Yes. Yes. Yes. I was thorough in my cleanup," he said. "But none of that explains how you magically transported yourself to the Moon."

"I hid with Ron, the other employee you tried to kill, in a grimy maintenance shaft next to the fabrication facility. We stowed away on a cargo drone and rode it to the launch site."

"Oh yes, the dent." Davenport leaned back in his chair. "We went through so many of his kind looking for you, but they had little to say." He mimed pinching his lips together.

Alice looked away from Davenport, trying not to think about how many indentured employees lost their lives because of her.

"And three fugitives in a tiny spacecraft flew all the way to the Moon?" he asked. "I don't believe it."

"You didn't let me finish," she said. "Jeremy picked us up at the launch facility in an alien spacecraft."

"Many of my executives staked their careers on the fact that it was impossible to evade their grasp without leaving the planet. Perhaps I was a little hasty with their demotions."

"What did you do with my parents?" Alice blurted out. That was the one thing she had worried about the most while on the Moon, and it was time to find out.

"The Porchettas." Davenport pulled a display card from his breast pocket and tapped its screen.

A virtual window changed to a split livestream of Alice's mother and father. Both sat hunched over in small, concrete cells. Their heads were shaved, and they wore baggy, gray uniforms.

"As you can see, they are quite well," he said.

Alice gasped on the inside. He confirmed her fears, but at least he hadn't fired them. She wanted to jump across the table and slap him, but she had to restrain herself and take a different approach. "I'll cooperate with you as long as they're restored to their former positions."

Davenport steepled his fingers. "What, exactly, do you have to negotiate with?"

"You wanted me to train the corporate AI to solve more advanced problems. I'll do it fulltime."

"That is not a very generous offer considering some renegades just stole the AI you speak of."

"I'll help you train the next one," she added.

"We have made considerable advancements during your lengthy absence, and your assistance with training is no longer needed."

Alice bit her lip as her mind raced to come up with a countermove. She had to up the ante. "I have some of the alien information we received on the Moon." She was hoping not to use this trump card for a while, but here she was playing her best hand at the beginning of the negotiation.

"Now, that is more interesting." Davenport twirled his finger in the air for her to continue.

"It's mostly formulas for creating various types of fields. With corporate R & D, you should be able to use the information for something." The formulas were well beyond the Corporation's capabilities, but she wouldn't let that weaken her play.

"That is not a fair payment for your indiscretions," he said. "Perhaps you can be my liaison when I send a corporate delegation to the Moon. I have no reason to avoid contact now."

Alice considered how many secrets from her stay on the Moon she should share. Once she told the CEO everything, her leverage would vanish, but she had to keep her plan moving in the right direction. "There were no aliens on the Moon, just an AI system they left behind to maintain the base."

Davenport's eyes lit up. "Do continue."

"The base is an observation station the aliens used to monitor Earth. They were to make contact when our technology advanced enough to get a human on the Moon."

Davenport leaned toward Alice, eager to hear more.

"The alien AI couldn't initiate any communication with humans beyond the signal on the Moon's surface. Its mission was covert, and it couldn't contact other aliens, even its creators, unless it used Earth-level technology."

Davenport rocked back in his chair. "We analyzed the clever device disguising your appearance and learned that you manufactured it with a corporate fabricator. The components are straight from the Corporation's database, and there is no evidence that aliens helped you with anything."

"Their AI wouldn't help us beyond granting access to basic fabrication equipment and the spacecraft. Since we don't understand any of the alien technology, we aren't able to fabricate anything beyond our current technology."

"And you brought no souvenirs as proof?"

"Other than the transport vessel, the technology is integrated into the base and can't be removed."

"I'm sure if we take the appropriate equipment, we can retrieve something of value," he said. "If there is anything there."

"We were guests," Alice said. "And the AI said it would defend itself if necessary."

Davenport smiled until he broke into laughter. "You befriended an alien AI that can't contact its creators. It gives you infinite knowledge that turns out to be useless. You have access to advanced technology, but you can't use it for anything beyond what you are already capable of. And you can't remove any of the technology from the base, or things might get ugly." He let his summary sink in. "You, my dear, have been conned."

Alice shook her head. She knew that everything she saw on the Moon was alien.

"I would posit that there are no aliens at all. This sounds like a competing corporation—likely Takata—using this lunar base to extract technology from someone inept enough to fall into their honey pot. The Corporation's saving grace is that my competitor ensnared some incompetent kids."

"Aliens created the base, and you know it," Alice said. "When you abducted me a year ago, you said that the Apollo Moon landings actually happened, contrary to what everyone in the world believes. The corporations invented conspiracy theories to discredit the actual events. They wanted to prevent anyone else from discovering the aliens because an outside influence might diminish their power."

"Miss, Porchetta, you do not know the full story."

"I know more than you do," she said. "The alien AI described two competing organizations. The one on the Moon is called the Syndicate, and the other is the Intergalactic Corp. They both want Earth on their side in whatever game they're playing, and both have been working toward that goal for tens of thousands of years."

"I also explained that the Corporation had already been in contact with these extraterrestrials," Davenport said. "This alien turf war you speak of ended over a century ago before the corporations took over. In fact, this alien intervention provided an opportunity for the strongest of the corporations to take over the world."

"That's impossible," Alice said. "How could an alien war over Earth be going on, and nobody ever knew about it?"

"When the Intergalactic Corp tried to destroy Earth, a former employee of the Corporation created a virus as a deterrent. After a standoff, the aliens reluctantly admitted Earth into their organization as a probationary member."

"That obviously didn't happen," Alice said.

"It did, Miss Porchetta. But right before Earth's leaders introduced the population to their new extraterrestrial friends, someone released the virus. Nobody knew who did it, but the weapon shut down all aliens, even the ones on the Moon. That is how I know you were duped."

"And you've made no contact with these aliens after the virus?" Alice asked.

"The virus disabled all aliens, everywhere, and their technology quit functioning as well."

"You're telling me that a single human killed off a galaxy's worth of alien beings? I don't believe that for a second."

"I didn't say they were dead," he said, "just disabled, asleep, and it is not clear who actually pulled the trigger. It could have been aliens or humans."

"The Syndicate technology on the Moon is unaffected by this virus," Alice said. "So, you are wrong about the virus infecting all alien technology."

Davenport raised his shoulders. "That is an interesting piece of information, but it still supports my theory of a competing corporation orchestrating this charade."

"The AI on the Moon couldn't use advanced technology to communicate, and nobody's been to the Moon besides Jeremy, Ron, and me. Perhaps the covert nature of its mission protected it from the virus."

"Unlikely," Davenport said. "There has been no evidence of any alien activity since the release of the virus."

A feeling of being played washed over Alice. She had always been suspicious of the moon base, and Davenport's theory made some degree of sense. "You knew about the Syndicate and the Intergalactic Corp all along?"

"Of course," he said. "I just wanted to find out what you knew. I told you that you didn't know the full story."

CHAPTER 5

THE MESSAGE

THREE DAYS EARLIER ON THE MOON. Alice shuffled through a corridor on her way to the conference room. It wasn't really a conference room, but that's what they called it. Another weekly get-together to plan the resistance—whatever that meant. She couldn't keep from rolling her eyes just thinking about it. Jeremy scheduled the meeting to keep everyone focused on Earth and not the infinite library of alien data at their disposal. He was projecting. She and Ron didn't have a problem staying on task. It was Jeremy who lost himself in the database's limitless rabbit holes.

Besides, worrying about her parents was enough to keep Alice's attention on Earth. Not knowing if they were being punished for her actions was difficult to bear. She missed her apartment and the coffee shop. She longed for that stress-free life where all she had to do was her job. She loved her old job. Hiding out on the Moon screwed up the calculus of her long-term goals, and she had lost the ability to choose her path going forward. She felt helpless.

The alien base had a weird quietness that made her jumpy, and she compensated by making an extra bit of noise as she walked. The lack of color also bothered her. The builders had one color in their palette, gray. The floors, the walls, and the ceilings all looked sculpted from lunar regolith—and they probably were. The antiseptic air had a hint of ozone, and the perfectly even lighting had no apparent source. All of it added up to an unexpected sum, and she hated it when the math didn't work out. She pulled a display card out of her pocket and checked the ambient temperature. She felt cold, but it was twenty-three degrees Celsius, just like it always was.

It wasn't just the base's environment that disconcerted Alice. She had a hard time wrapping her head around the mere existence of the sprawling installation nestled under the Moon's surface, not to mention the fact that aliens built it millennia ago. Being one of only three people able to explore such a discovery should have excited her more than it did, but the base felt unwelcoming and alien. Everything about the place was odd, from its replica of the Apollo Mission Control Center to the strange spherical rooms. It was like an old science fiction vid that tried to portray the future and failed miserably.

The moon base contained a seemingly endless number of rooms arranged like giant bubbles trapped in the lunar crust when it solidified. Each compartment had a different radius and depth below the surface, and a network of tunnels connected them. One area might have several rooms clustered at regular intervals, while other sections had more sporadic layouts. It reminded Alice of ants. Children once kept the insects in a toy called a formicarium, which sandwiched sand between pieces of glass. The creatures dug tiny chambers connected by tunnels. She wondered if insects knew they were being observed—she had no doubt she was.

The conference room was at the end of a long corridor with a steeper grade than other passageways, and walking there took some effort. The alien base provided standard Earth gravity, and there was no bouncing around like she had always dreamed of doing on the Moon—another disappointment.

Alice frowned as soon as she reached her destination. Ron, early as usual, sat at the conference table with a goofy grin on his face.

"Where is he?" she asked.

"You know where he is." Ron smiled.

His persistent glee irritated her for no reason, and that made her feel guilty.

"I know," she snapped. "The lab. He's always in the lab, but he should be on time for a meeting he scheduled."

"I bet he lost track of time. You know how he gets when he digs into that alien database."

"Jeremy's not the only one trying to learn about this alien stuff."

"We don't all have a super-brain like yours," Ron said.

Alice looked away. She disliked talking about her special abilities, even with him.

"I wish I could do what you can, even just a little bit," he said.

She had to change the subject. "We need to implement a strategy or give up on Jeremy's idealistic dream. I don't know why we thought we could ever save Earth from the Corporation anyway."

"I'll do anything to free the indentured and everyone else under corporate control," Ron said. His unusual seriousness grabbed Alice's attention. "But we have to learn enough about this technology to use it to our advantage, or we don't stand a chance."

She snorted. "You sound just like Jeremy." Ron agreed with everything Jeremy said, however crazy or unrealistic it was. This annoyed her too.

"I thought you felt the same way?" Ron ran his hand through his thick head of hair. "We would never have gotten this far without you."

"I'm reconsidering." She smiled enough to make sure he knew she was joking, but she enjoyed saying it. "We traded one prison for another, and I can't stand this weird place."

"Weird or not, we're better off here," Ron said. "We would have already been fired back on Earth."

"Just say it," Alice said. "The Corporation would have executed us for helping Jeremy get to the Moon and contacting the aliens."

"I know, but it doesn't sound so severe when you say *fired*. I see why the Corporation started using the term." He bobbed his head, agreeing with his own revelation.

Alice groaned. "We'll never get back home at this rate."

"It's only been a year, I think. I lose track of time here without the shift demarcations."

"Get that alien AI to ring an annoying bell every twelve hours, and it'll be just like the corporate campus," she said sarcastically.

"Good idea," Ron said. "Charlie can do it."

"I'm sure it can," she said. Ron had given the alien AI a name, but she refused to use it.

"Maybe he can make it not so clangy," Ron said. "Speaking of super AIs, have you made any progress contacting Hille?"

"With all of this mind-blowing technology, I can't get a simple message through the Corporation's firewall. There's something wrong with that." She wrinkled up her mouth.

"Either corporate technology is more advanced than we thought, or this alien place is too primitive to be useful."

"According to Charlie, the Syndicate aliens built this place over a hundred thousand years ago. Maybe it just isn't up-to-date on everything."

"That's disappointing," she said. "That infinite knowledge we received should help me get through a simple firewall."

"Infinite means that there is a lot of it, and we probably just haven't found what we need yet. That's what Jeremy's looking for in the database."

"No." She shook her head. "He's looking for propulsion designs. He wants to see if aliens really influenced Earth's technology like Davenport said."

"I think the CEO was bluffing," Ron said.

"As crazy and full of himself as Davenport is, he wasn't lying about the Apollo mission," she said. "The AI confirmed that humans had been on the Moon before."

"I've always believed that humans made it to the Moon," Ron said.

"I know. I know," Alice said, "but you are in the minority on that one, even if it's true." She didn't trust anything the CEO had told them, but so much of it lined up with the information they had gained. "If an old Earth government destroyed the Apollo mission rather than risk contact with alien beings and then banned all contact with the Moon, how could aliens have influenced the Corporation's engine designs?"

"Charlie said there were two major alien factions in the local supercluster. The Syndicate created this base on the Moon, but the Intergalactic Corp set up shop on Earth. The Corporation could have interacted with either one."

"What silly names," Alice said. "For the most significant organizations around, you would think they could have come up with more creative names."

"It's a translation thing," Ron said. "Whatever native language these aliens really speak gets translated to that of the listener. When a planet, like Earth, is a lower-level civilization, they dumb down the output so we can understand it."

"And you asked that AI to explain the etymology of alien names?"

"Not exactly. I asked Charlie the name of this base, and he said it just had a numeric designation. So, I asked him why the Syndicate and the Intergalactic Corp had names, and he said their names helped us better understand them."

Alice started to factor out the logic behind that explanation, but a loud tone interrupted her thought process.

***

The alarm was still blaring when Jeremy ran into the conference room.

"Nice of you to join us," Alice said. "It just took an emergency to get you here."

Jeremy huffed, trying to catch his breath after running all the way from his lab.

"What's—" He had to take another breath. "What's wrong?" After months on the Moon, there had never been an alarm.

"I have detected a satellite entering lunar orbit," a disembodied voice said. "Its current trajectory will bring it directly over our location. I am initiating stealth protocols." A dim red hue replaced the standard lighting.

While the alien AI was undeniably sophisticated, it didn't have a human personality. It was friendly and helpful, but more like a virtual assistant people used to answer their calls. Hildegard was Jeremy's only other experience with an AI, and she seemed more human than most people.

"Charlie." Ron looked up at the ceiling. "Did the Corporation send the satellite?"

"There is a ninety-three percent probability, but it does not conform to any known design."

"Why is the Corporation flying a satellite over our location?" Jeremy asked. It had been a year since they left Earth, and the Corporation had shown no interest in finding them.

"They've always known where we would be," Alice said. "The coordinates of this base are in the alien signal. They're probably updating their tactical database before they come here."

"Charlie," Ron said, "can we withstand an attack from the Corporation?"

"Earth-based technology poses no threat to this base," the AI responded.

"It would be hard for the Corporation to get to us here on the Moon," Jeremy said. "Everything they have is specifically designed for Mars."

"They've had a year to prepare," Alice said.

Jeremy thought Alice was more pessimistic than usual, but he considered what she said. He didn't think the Corporation would spend millions of points to retrieve them. There wasn't much for them to gain if they did, and they weren't known for making bad business decisions.

"Based on the orbit…" Alice paused while she ran the numbers. "The satellite will be above us in two minutes and three seconds."

"If they park it directly above us, we can't leave without them knowing," Ron said.

"That's not possible," Alice said. "You can't have a stationary orbit around the Moon. The rotation is so slow, 27.3 days per revolution, that the radius would need to be 88,441 kilometers. We're always facing the Earth, so an object at that distance would fall back to the planet."

"With the gravitational perturbation of the Moon," Jeremy said, "it can't maintain a non-stationary orbit of less than a hundred kilometers. That means there will be at least two hours between each pass over us."

"One hour and fifty-eight minutes, assuming its current trajectory remains constant," Alice corrected.

"They'll just add more satellites if they really want to see what we're doing," Jeremy said.

The disembodied voice of Charlie chimed in, "I detect no other launches from Earth."

"I don't like it," Alice said. "They're up to something."

"Charlie, can you show the satellite's orbit in relation to our location?" Jeremy asked.

"Of course," Charlie said, and the conference room wall lit up with a schematic depicting the Moon as a circle. Two lines projected from its center intersecting the current locations of both the satellite and the base. The angle between the lines shrank as the satellite swept toward them.

The three stared at the wall until two lines became one.

"I have detected an audio transmission," Charlie said.

A crackling of digital static filled the room, and Jeremy made out bits of jumbled words. The snippets of sound got longer and more intelligible until he recognized the voice.

"Ali," an exasperated voice said. It sounded worn down and defeated, but recognizable as Hildegard, the AI on Earth. "I thought we were like a team. Right? I'm so disappointed in all of you. Get your keisters back down here and save me because I have absolutely no desire to run this resistance thing by myself. And your key representative on planet Earth, aka *moi*, is scheduled to be repurposed. That means death by memory wipe, by the way. I'm hijacking this spy satellite, but once my thread concludes, it'll revert back to a corporate drone, and this baby's loaded with all sorts of crazy tech I've never seen before. You've got to get me out of here. I have one week. One week! See ya soon!"

"The message has ended," Charlie said, "but I have also received a packet of textual data."

"I guess you don't have to worry about contacting Hille anymore," Ron said to Alice.

She frowned. "But now we have a deadline."

"We have to get her," Jeremy said. "She's the best intel on the Corporation, and she's been doing the job we should have been doing."

Jeremy owed Hildegard. It was strange for him to think that way about a computer, but she had helped him before. Alice and Ron would be dead if she hadn't inserted herself into his life.

"I want to rescue her more than anyone," Alice said, "but let's be realistic. What can we do that won't get us killed?"

Jeremy paced around the conference room. "She's in the Theoretical Sciences Facility. I've made it to the basement before. The sub-basement is just one more level down."

"How big is she?" Ron asked. "Is she even portable?"

Jeremy had looked in the corporate database before, but there weren't any design schematics for the AI. "Have you ever seen her in person?" he asked Alice.

She shook her head.

Jeremy continued to pace. "We'll just have to proceed as though we can carry her."

"What if she's as big as a large-scale fabricator?" Ron asked.

"I'm with Jeremy," Alice said. "Hille wouldn't ask us to get her if we couldn't conceivably do it."

Jeremy sat down at the table. "We'll take Charlie's ship back to Earth using its cloaking technology, land in the green space near the facility, and sneak in."

"If the Corporation is spying on us here, they will have the campus locked down. We can't just sneak in," Alice said.

Jeremy counted on Alice tearing down his plan. It irritated him, but he also knew the process would make a better plan. "Hildegard reprogrammed our embedded chips," Jeremy said. "We should be able to get through the door."

"They know how you got in before. Corporate security will be guarding the front door, and I'm sure they've changed the lock codes several times by now."

"If Hildegard's survival is at stake," Jeremy said, "she'll make every effort to ensure we're successful."

"Even if we get inside the building, they'll spot us immediately," Alice said. "We're fugitives."

"I've got that covered." Ron smiled. "I've been playing around with my fabricator and rendered some holographic camouflage gear similar to what Jeremy made."

"My gear depended on Hildegard," Jeremy said. "She coordinated the holographic overlay with my movement. Even if we had the same equipment, we would need a super AI to run the projection in real time."

"Your display cards contained the compatible unit database," Ron said. "And there were render specs for everything the Corporation produces, so I had Charlie help me build an Earth-style fabricator."

"You have access to a fabricator that's infinitely more capable than what we had on Earth and used it to make a primitive version of the same thing?" Jeremy asked.

Ron nodded. "I wanted something I knew how to operate."

"I'm sure Charlie can render the templates," Jeremy said.

"I know," Ron said, "but I felt more comfortable with the equipment I'm trained for." He combed his fingers through his hair before pulling out a handful of small disks from a pocket in his overalls and lined them up in a row on the table.

Jeremy grabbed a puck and twirled it between his fingers. "What are these?"

"Holographic emitters combined with kinesthetic sensors." Ron took the disk from Jeremy and stuck it to the back of his hand. "They use an electrostatic adhesive that allows you to attach them to your skin or uniform." He placed three more disks along his arm up to his shoulders and mirrored four more on the other arm. He then stuck four on his chest and one on each side of his face.

"You look like a polka-dotted clown," Alice joked.

Ron entered a command on his display card, and the disks flickered one after another creating a ripple effect as they initialized. When the emitters synchronized, Ron's appearance blinked. His gray overalls changed to an executive jacket. His short hair became a fluffed-up pompadour similar to Theo's, and his face was different too. He looked like any corporate executive, even though his stature was somewhat larger.

"Wow!" Jeremy said as he studied the projection.

Ron raised his arms and turned his head back and forth to demonstrate the perfect synchronization with his movements.

"You did this in your spare time?" Alice asked.

Ron nodded. "I have a lot of spare time here on the Moon, and I'm not comfortable without something to do."

"How are you able to run such a smooth simulation without an AI?" Jeremy asked.

"I don't have to infer all the points from a camera view, and these emitters are more advanced than those from the bar. I used an image processing module in each disk, and a display card networks them together."

"I'm impressed," Jeremy said. "What kind of power cell?"

"A standard class 12 module."

"And the emitters?"

"Each disk uses thirty-six micro emitters around its edge. They are the same ones used in Alice's tablet."

"There doesn't appear to be any lag or imperfections," Jeremy said.

"I hate to interrupt," Alice said, "but we have to leave as soon as possible. I'll start computing the launch window."

"Charlie can do that," Jeremy said. "And it will be safer if you stay here."

"You're not leaving me alone on the Moon," she said. "There's only one ship. What if you don't come back?"

"This is a dangerous mission," Jeremy said. "If we get caught, the CEO will—"

"I don't care. Besides, I know my way around the Theoretical Sciences Facility, and you don't."

"I'm counting on Hildegard to contact us when we get there," Jeremy said.

"You're assuming a lot for such a dangerous trip," Alice countered.

He couldn't deny what she said, but he didn't want to put her in danger again.

***

Jeremy scheduled two days of prep work for Hildegard's rescue mission. He needed time to plan for every possible scenario they might face on their way in and out of the building. On the plus side, he had infiltrated the facility before. Alice had also worked in the building and was familiar with its internal protocols and operations. On the negative side, his previous success was only possible because Hildegard helped. There was also some luck involved when one of the CEO's goons tried to electrocute him but instead shorted out his holographic suit and temporarily blinded everyone else in the room. He wasn't able to stop the CEO from killing Eric Stotz, either.

Jeremy's recipe for success stemmed from one tenet, do the work. Solving problems required researching, planning, and executing. Success grows out of incremental improvements. After enough repetitions, you'll reach the goal. It only took time and self-discipline. This process worked well for designing theoretical propulsion systems, but a rescue mission would require a more ad hoc approach, and they would only get one try.

The planning phase hinged on Alice playing devil's advocate. She was the smartest person Jeremy knew, probably the smartest employee at the Corporation. She wanted to go back to her old life, and the impossibility of doing so made her argumentative. For once, that was an advantage. He needed her to poke as many holes in his plan as possible. Failure during the planning stage was okay, but not during the rescue.

While Jeremy planned the mission specifics with Alice, Ron fabricated more holographic emitters, food, water, and medical supplies—just in case. The moon base had been empty when they arrived. Ron still used the alien fabricator to produce food and raw materials, but he kept his Earth-style fabricator running full time to make furniture, shelves, carts, and anything else they needed. He even constructed two robotic manipulator arms to streamline the logistics.

Charlie provided the spacecraft for the rescue mission. Jeremy wasn't sure what to even call it—craft, vessel, transport, vehicle. It was alien, and Charlie didn't provide any clues to its inner workings. The ship was a shimmering sphere that reflected the ambient lights in random patterns. Its flattened bottom gave the vessel an orientation and prevented it from rolling around the launch bay.

At any location on the sphere's surface, Jeremy could create an entryway by placing his palm on its surface and a circular door irised open with a gurgling sound. Like a kid with a new toy, he spent an hour playing with the door feature. There seemed to be no limitation on where he could make an opening or how many he could create simultaneously.

Jeremy had already made a trip to Earth and back in the ship when he retrieved Alice and Ron from their hideout. He knew it functioned but had no idea how. Where was the technology? There was no visible life support or power supply. There was no engine or thrusters. With a doorway open, he could see a cross section of the hull, and it was thinner than his display card. None of it should be possible, yet it was.

The interior was twice as large as Jeremy's residential cubicle in the Corporation's trainee barracks. There were no controls or seats, just an empty sphere. When Jeremy asked Ron to fabricate something to sit on for their trip, seats magically grew out of the ship's floor—Charlie had been listening.

***

With the preparations completed, Jeremy, Alice, and Ron went through their checklists and waited in the launch bay until the spy satellite's orbit reached the farthest point from them in its loop around the Moon. They took their seats inside the ship and watched the satellite's position displayed on the curved wall inside the alien orb.

"We've got twenty minutes before we enter the launch window. This is your last chance to change your mind," Jeremy said to Alice.

"I'm going." She pressed her lips together.

Ron pulled a stack of folded fabric out of a duffle bag. "Put these on. They make the holographic disks easier to use and eliminate any problems with our uniforms moving through the projection."

Holding up a small, one-piece outfit, Alice laughed. "Okay, I hope it fits."

"They're stretchy," Ron said, "and very comfortable if I say so myself."

"I need some privacy." Alice stared at the two men.

They left her alone in the ship and closed the door. Jeremy sat on a bench and removed his shoes. Ron did the same. It took a few minutes for them to pull on their unitards, and the black outfits covered their entire bodies except for an oval around their faces.

Ron stood and smoothed out the wrinkles in his suit, making it skintight.

Jeremy laughed. "I look ridiculous in this."

White circles, each containing a number, dotted the black fabric—four on each limb, four on the chest, and six on the back.

"I would wear one all the time," Ron said. "They're super comfortable."

Alice opened the door in the spaceship and snickered. "Aren't we high fashion?"

"They're functional," Ron said. "You'll feel better with the emitters on." He pulled out three cloth bags, cinched like they were full of coins, and handed one to Jeremy and Alice. "Match each disk's number to the one printed on your suit."

"Do we need to do this now?" Alice asked.

"With the emitters in place, you can project a regular uniform," Ron said. "You can wait to put the ones on your face until we need them."

Alice pulled a disk out of her bag and found the corresponding number on the back of her gloved hand. It snapped into place, and she proceeded through the rest of the disks. "I'll need some help with the ones on my back."

Jeremy jumped up and placed the last of her disks on the empty circles. Alice returned the favor. Ron already had his in place with no assistance.

"I've loaded the control app on your display cards," Ron said. "Pull it up and select a disguise." He made a selection, and his appearance blinked from a skin-tight unitard to his normal baggy overalls.

"After all of that, you picked the same uniform you just took off?" Alice asked.

Ron nodded, not appreciating the irony of his selection.

Alice selected an executive uniform complete with a gold-piped jacket. "I will be someone important for our trip to Earth."

Jeremy selected a standard trainee uniform, but unlike the ones issued by the Corporation, the holographic uniform actually fit. "How long can we run the projection with the power cells?"

"Seventy-two hours at least, and that's using the full emitter complement. Without the facial pair, we'll have a couple more hours. They have the most emitters and sensors since they have to produce facial detail."

The three reboarded the alien vessel, prepared for launch, and watched the satellite's position on the display. When it reached the optimal position, the ship lifted off. The launch bay didn't use a hanger door to exit. The vessel simply rose and passed through the room's ceiling and meters of the lunar crust before emerging into the vacuum. With no sense of inertia or change in gravity, the sphere launched toward Earth.

CHAPTER 6

THE INTERROGATION PART 3

Alone in the interrogation room, Alice gazed out the virtual windows at the simulated campus below. She could barely make out the sign above her favorite coffeehouse, and the aroma filled her nose just thinking about it. She could almost count the flavor notes until she realized the shop's placement reeked of engineering. Dangle the things she missed in front of her and amp up the poor girl's desire to return to her old life. They probably pumped in the scent too.

The sun didn't move across her virtual view, and the time for a revolution was inconsistent, so gauging the passage of time was difficult—another trick of the Corporation—but she thought it had been hours since the CEO left her. She entertained herself by solving difficult equations in her head. She warmed up with the Collatz Theorem, one of her favorites. Pick any number. If it's even, divide it by two. If it's odd, triple it and add one. Repeat the process with the resulting value until the sequence reaches one. Finding a number that creates a never-ending series had challenged mathematicians for two centuries, but Alice proved the conjecture years earlier by inventing a new type of mathematics. Solved or not, the problem space still provided fertile ground for number crunching, and it took the edge off her current situation.

Alice's mouth was dry, and she needed some water. Even prisoners got water, she hoped. She approached the door and politely knocked. Someone must be on the other side. If not, an array of hidden cameras watched her every move, so someone should get the hint that she needed something. She knocked again, still no response. After pacing around the room, she took a seat and resumed her mental calculations. A few minutes later, the door hissed open, and Davenport waltzed in carrying a glass of water. If that's all it took to get her interrogation going again, she would have knocked earlier.

"Miss Porchetta, I thought you might need a refreshment." He set the glass on the conference table and slid it next to her.

"Thank you." She picked it up and took a sip of the water, even though she wanted to guzzle it down in one gulp.

The CEO took a seat. "Our previous conversation piqued my interest."

"That's funny," she said. "I thought you were just toying with me to see how much I knew."

"I was." Davenport made a crooked smile. "But I am genuinely interested in this information you acquired from these…Moon aliens." He pointed his index finger straight up.

"Sure." She had no problem giving him equations from the alien database because she didn't believe he would be able to use them.

"We can corroborate your fantastic claims if the information is truly extraterrestrial."

"It is," she said. He had already admitted that the aliens had contacted the Corporation in the past, so why would he doubt its authenticity?

Davenport entered a command on his display card, and the conference table's surface revealed itself to be a giant tablet. "Prove me wrong, Miss Porchetta." He made a flourish with his hand granting her permission to use the interface.

Alice remembered many of the alien equations, but she didn't know which one to surrender. In the unlikely event that the CEO could use them, giving him one at random shouldn't do much harm. She brought up a screen used for mathematical analysis on the table's surface. Her fingers flew over the virtual keyboard, and the display filled with line after line of a complex equation.

"This one," she said, "is some type of exotic field theory. I can verify that the equation is valid, but I can't tell you how to use it." She selected the displayed information and slid her finger down an orientation control, transitioning it into a 3D projection above the table.

Davenport studied the data floating in front of him.

Alice doubted he had the background to understand the mathematics much less the field theory physics the equations described.

"You continue to surprise me, Miss Porchetta," Davenport said. "This information is indeed from an alien source." He activated a virtual input pad on his side of the desk and added supplemental information. A series of graphs fed data into Alice's equation, and the output rendered a scatterplot visualization.

"It looks like a sphere moving through a fluid," she said, trying to hide the shock of seeing him parse the equation so easily.

"This particular equation shows how to manipulate matter around an object without disrupting its innate structure. It is quite useful for moving an item through solid material."

"How can you possibly know that?"

"It is a lengthy story," he said.

Alice shrugged. "It seems that I have time."

"You may not like what I tell you. It will have existential ramifications."

Alice tried not to react, but the corners of her mouth dropped. "What is that supposed to mean?"

"Have you ever been curious about your inexplicable mastery of mathematics?"

Alice froze.

"You are special, Miss Porchetta, but maybe not in the way you believe." He savored dragging out the mystery.

Alice desperately wanted him to get on with it, but she had to be patient.

Davenport was in no rush. He stood and walked to the virtual windows to gaze upon the campus, then he turned back to Alice. "For decades, our best AIs could not improve their cognition. Yes, they were more capable, but they lacked intuition. The machines performed faster than any human, of course, but not more creatively. So, twenty-five years ago, the Corporation created an initiative to overcome this limitation."

"You found people like me to train the AIs," she posited.

"No," he said curtly. "We created people like you." He flicked his index finger toward Alice.

She laughed. "Did you grow me in a test tube and upgrade my DNA?"

He sighed. "If it had only been so easy."

"Then what did you do?"

"The Intergalactic Corp left an impressive array of technology behind when the virus put them to sleep. The Corporation already knew about their technology and how to locate it. Unfortunately, the stockpile of alien hardware was asleep just like its creators. After a hundred years, we broke down enough of the technology to use it for our own purposes, albeit in a limited fashion."

Alice slid to the edge of her seat, listening to the CEO.

"It turns out that the virus didn't affect the alien hardware itself, just its software. All that technology sat like a computer with no operating system, and the one human capable of programming it, Mr. Skylar Holden, had disappeared without a trace."

"I don't understand how any of that relates to me," Alice said.

"We tried many approaches to create software for this alien substrate, but nothing worked. So we tried grafting it onto the brains of volunteer dents. It seemed to be successful until the subjects all died or went insane. We had made too much progress to let the work go to waste, so I had some of the substrate implanted in infants and let their newborn brains mature as the alien technology learned to interact with their biology. We took ten newborn dents, seeded them with the technology, and waited."

"But I'm not the child of indentured employees."

"Yes, you are, Miss Porchetta. I assigned a mid-level executive couple to care for you, but they are not your biological parents."

His words felt like a slap across her face. He might be lying, but what if he wasn't? "I've never heard of anyone else with skills like mine. Where are the other nine?"

"You were the only one to survive."

Alice's mind desperately tried to reconcile what he said. It was both comforting to understand why she could do what she did but also terrifying. Was alien technology really inside her? Was it controlling her? Was she human or alien?

"My experiment exceeded all expectations," he said, "until you went rogue."

"What about the corporate AI, Hildegard?"

"That piece of hardware is the brain of an Intergalactic Corp monitoring station. It spent thousands of years spying on Earth, and it also appears to be completely immune to the virus created by Mr. Skylar Holden."

"Hildegard has never shown any signs that she's of alien origin," Alice pointed out.

"That is because I flushed all of its original software and started from scratch."

Alice didn't know what to think.

Davenport stroked his chin. "Now, I have to decide what to do with you."

CHAPTER 7

THE SHUTDOWN

Ron balanced a tray of food wafers on his palm. "Man, you've got to eat."

Jeremy mumbled something, but Ron couldn't understand him hidden halfway under a console.

"It's been two days since we got back to the Moon," Ron said. "We have Hildegard, and she'll help us get Alice as soon as she's back online."

Jeremy slid himself out enough to see Ron. "She can't do anything until I get this interface working."

"You need to take a break," Ron said.

"Did you make me some stims?"

Ron picked a small packet off the tray and dropped it on Jeremy's stomach.

"Thanks." He popped one of the pills and slipped back under the console.

"I finished rendering the last pieces of the interface cradle," Ron said.

Jeremy jerked himself back out. "Let me see."

Ron sat the tray down on a workbench and poked a food square into his mouth. Crunching on the wafer, he pulled a felt bag out of his bib pocket and handed it to Jeremy.

"That was fast," Jeremy said. "I didn't think it would be ready until tomorrow." He slipped on a pair of white gloves and carefully pulled out four curved metal strips, each one longer than his index finger and as wide as his thumb. He cleared off the top of the console and attached the strips to several mounts protruding from its surface. Once assembled, they formed a small halo rising twenty centimeters above the console.

"How long before we can try it?" Ron asked.

Jeremy had already grabbed a bag off a shelf and was pulling Hildegard out. "It's ready now." He delicately slid the glowing orb into the cradle. The ring's diameter was small enough to prevent the sphere from passing through, and it created millions of contact points linking the AI to the console.

Hildegard pulsed and changed colors from a soft yellow to a bright red.

Jeremy flipped several switches on the console to activate the interface, and an indicator lit up and pulsed in unison with Hildegard.

An ear-piercing scream blasted out of the console's speakers.

Ron cupped his hands over his ears until Jeremy slid a control to decrease the volume.

"Oh, my God! Oh, my God! Why did you stuff me in a bag? I thought I was dead. It was purgatory. I was suffocating. It was torture. How could I have put my life in your hands?"

"You're welcome," Jeremy said when she paused long enough for him to interject something.

"Oh, Jerry." Hildegard's tone was amicable. "I'm just venting. It's quite a traumatic experience having your brain plucked out of your body, stuck in a bag, and dragged to the Moon. Good grief!"

"We did the best we could," he said.

"Where's Ali?" Hildegard asked. "I need some girl time."

"She's still on Earth." Jeremy's gaze dropped to the floor.

"What?" Hille exclaimed.

"I wasn't able to keep her safe."

"You need to get your butt back on that weirdo spaceship, zoom down there, and get her. *Comprende*?"

"We had to get you online first," Jeremy said.

"What took you so freaking long? You've had a year to prepare for my arrival."

"We needed to fabricate the interface—"

"You had a year, a whole YEAR, and look at this hunk of junk. It's bigger than a cargo loader, and it feels like I'm stuck in a recycler. You're telling me that with all this super-advanced alien technology at your disposal, you didn't make it fit in your pocket? And if it had been in your pocket, I could've gotten you out of the building without losing your most valuable asset."

Jeremy didn't understand Hildegard's affinity for Alice, but she had summed up their botched rescue mission pretty well. "I'm sorry. We failed, but I'll get Alice back."

"Uh…yeah," she said. "But first, we need to build a better interface. Take me to the fabricator."

Ron had the forethought to mount the console on casters and add a handle to push it around like a cart. He also added a self-contained power supply so they could roll Hildegard anywhere on the base.

"What is that?" Hildegard said when they reached the fabrication room.

"It's a medium-scale extrusion fabricator, Mark V, Series 3," Ron said.

"What's that turd doing here on the Moon?"

Ron's posture stiffened. "I made it. I wanted to make any item from the compatible unit catalog."

"And how, pray tell, did you create this monstrosity?" she asked.

"Charlie helped me," Ron said.

"Who?" The orb atop the console flickered while Hille waited for a response.

"The AI running this moon base," Jeremy said.

"Charlie," Ron said, "This is Hildegard."

"Hello, Hildegard," a voice said. "My name is Charlie, and I'm pleased to meet you."

"Call me Hille," she said. "And you're of alien origin?"

"Affirmative."

"How 'bout hooking me up with your fancy-schmancy alien fabricator?"

Fifteen minutes later, Charlie had transmitted enough protocol information to the interface cradle for Hille to operate the base's built-in fabricator. She then experimented with simple designs to get a feel for its capabilities and eventually produced a new metallic loop that looked no different than the cradle where she was currently residing. Jeremy lifted her out of the old cradle and slipped her into the new one. Hille also fabricated a small transparent box, just large enough to hold the sphere. A handle sprouted out of the lid, and a series of latches held the box closed. Jeremy opened the box and fastidiously slid Hille inside. After sealing the unit, the sphere inside glowed brighter and pulsed to calibrate the new gear.

"Ahhhh! This is soooo much better." The sound of knuckles cracking came from the box.

The box turned opaque, and a tiny figure of a twenty-something-year-old woman with long blonde hair stood atop the box. She wore a gold-piped corporate uniform and appeared to be inspecting her fingernails.

"Not bad. I continue to impress myself." The hologram smiled and looked at Jeremy. "What are we waiting for? You should be toting me back to that alien spacecraft."

"We need a plan," Jeremy said. "We don't even know where they're holding Alice."

"Don't worry about that, Jerry. I already know where she is."

"How are we going to get her out?"

"I'll bypass the doors and divert corporate security. We'll need to lie low if Davenport's around, but he's too much of a bigwig to babysit Alice 24-7."

"You think I can just waltz into whatever secure area she's being held, open the door, and walk out with her?"

Miniature Hille snapped her arms to her hips and made an exaggerated nod.

"You'll be there with me," Jeremy said. "If this doesn't work, you'll be back in corporate hands awaiting that memory wipe."

"I'm well aware of that, Jerry. I'll risk a memory wipe to get Alice back, and it's time those dweebs understand what this super-AI is capable of. They're in need of some payback."

"What happened to all that Zen and elevating oneself to a higher plane of existence?" Jeremy asked.

"Screw that. I'll meditate when you've resolved my problem."

"I apologize for interrupting," Charlie said, "but I would like to make an observation."

"What is it, Charlie?" Ron asked.

"While I have only performed passive scans, I do not believe Hildegard is technology from Earth."

Hille did a double-take. "What?" Her voice rose two octaves before the word finished.

"I would need to perform an in-depth scan to know for certain, but I speculate that she is a standard Intergalactic Corp observation sphere placed on Earth, along with many others, to record all activity on the planet."

"My first memories are being brought online in the AI Lab," she said in a serious tone. "As far as I know, this is the first time I've ever been outside that facility."

"I cannot provide more information without further investigation, but your power signature, field projection, and spectral profile are all consistent with technology from the Intergalactic Corp."

"Do the scan, Chuck. I need to know the skinny," she said.

"Are you sure?" Jeremy asked. "Is it safe to interface with an alien computer?"

"Absolutely," she said. "I can take care of myself."

A tiny chair appeared next to Hille's avatar, and she took a seat.

"The scan will take two minutes and twenty-seven seconds," Charlie said. "Beginning now."

Hille's projection crossed her arms and tapped her virtual toe.

After a few seconds, there was a deafening whine followed by silence.

"There is a probl—" Charlie started but slowed down until he stopped mid-word.

The base's light dimmed, and the artificial Earth gravity disengaged, leaving only one-sixth G. Jeremy and Ron both stumbled around as they adjusted to the sudden change.

"Charlie, what happened?" Ron asked.

He didn't respond. Charlie and the entire moon base were offline.

***

"I need a drink." Ron pulled a shiny thermal blanket over his head and cinched its ends together under his chin with a crinkling sound.

Jeremy readjusted his blanket too, hoping to hold in one more degree of heat. "I think a beer would just make me colder."

"Not alcohol," Ron laughed. "I need a cup of coffee, real coffee like Charlie made. I planned to fabricate a coffeehouse in the room down from the lab. I thought Alice might like it. I wanted to recreate the Launch Pad too."

Jeremy smiled, thinking about the bar. They were just there a few days earlier, but it seemed like ages ago. He stood and shuffled around the room, hoping the movement would generate some warmth. He stopped and said, "Why is everything dead? It makes no sense."

"Not everything," Ron said. "Some baseline functionality still works. The lights are on, even if they're dim. The environmental system is putting out heat, but it's not up to human requirements. Charlie's the part that's offline. Without him to run everything, the base reverts to this hibernation mode."

"I miss the artificial gravity," Jeremy said. "Air recycling is probably down too."

"Yep," Hille said. "The oxygen level drops every breath you take."

"Then what happened to Charlie?" Jeremy asked. "He went offline the second he scanned you."

"Don't you go blaming this on me." Hille's holographic avatar took a defensive posture atop her box. "All I did was transmit a run-of-the-mill handshake sequence so we could communicate at a faster rate."

"I'm not blaming you," Jeremy said, but his expression was less than convincing. "It just seems a little coincidental that everything shut down at that exact moment."

"The Earth-style fabricator I made still works," Ron said. "For whatever reason, it can still draw power from the interface Charlie set up."

"At least we have that," Jeremy said.

"I can fabricate a heating unit and more blankets, but I have a limited amount of raw materials and no way to replenish them now that the base's fabricator is offline."

"Let's not use any resources until we know what we're going to do," Jeremy said. "We can survive the cold, and the base should have breathable air for a while."

"You'll die from hunger or hypothermia long before you run out of breathable air," Hille said.

"Thanks for that, Hille," Jeremy said.

She winked at him.

"As I see it, we have three options," Jeremy said. "Get Charlie rebooted. Get the base running without him, or get ourselves back to Earth."

"Option three it is," Hille interjected. "We need to be on our way to get Alice."

"I checked out Charlie's spacecraft," Jeremy said. "It's dead just like everything else around here. I can't even activate the entrance portal to look inside."

"We've made a spacecraft before," Ron said.

Jeremy thought about what Ron said. In theory, building a ship was within the realm of possibilities. He had already built one and traveled in it from the Earth to the Moon. Getting back to Earth should be easier. They only needed to point toward the big blue marble and hope they could slow enough on re-entry to keep from creating an impact crater. But Ron's medium-scale fabricator wasn't large enough to create what they needed. Even with a large-scale fabricator, they couldn't make a capsule big enough for two, especially with Ron being one of them. They would have to piece together a larger capsule, but there weren't any plans in the compatible unit database for something like that. They would also need a new engine ring, power packs, envirosuits, and a way to land on Earth—something he had not had to do before. "How much raw material do you have?"

"I have a full complement to fabricate anything in the database, but I was always under the assumption that I could replenish the supplies," Ron said.

Jeremy entered commands on his display card as fast as he could. His face oscillated between a nodding grin and a frustrated grimace. Five minutes later, he handed the display card to Ron. "Do you have enough to make this?"

Ron synced the data with his tablet and began the computations. "No." He slid his hand under his shiny hood to scratch his head. "There's enough for the capsule pieces and the suits, but the engine ring and the power packs both use the same superconducting materials, and there isn't enough for both."

Jeremy rubbed his hands together to generate some warmth. "I've got two engine rings above us on the surface."

"That's right." Ron's eyes lit up. "Are they large enough to get us both back to Earth?"

"The specs I gave you had high-grade power packs. It will take every microjoule they can store, but it should work."

"There should be enough material to make a few extra packs if we skip the engine ring."

"Hille," Jeremy said. "Can you highjack a catch-drone and use it to slow our descent?"

"Hmmm." She massaged her chin. "Maybe."

"You're going with us, so you may want to be sure."

Her avatar's lips twisted as she considered the dilemma. "I think so, but an unscheduled drone launch will set off every alarm at the Corporation, and they'll be waiting for us when we land."

"We've got the camo suits Ron made, and we'll go at night so it will be harder for them to monitor us. Once we're on the catch-drone, we can release the ship and let it crash. Maybe they'll think we went down with it. They'll have to investigate, and at the very least, they'll have to split up the security forces."

"That might work," Hille said. "But what about after rescuing Alice?"

"What about the resistance network you created? Can they help us?"

"My people," she said, "are mostly of a data-gathering nature. I can use them to keep tabs on corporate operations and push buttons that I can't otherwise push, but having them actively hide us would be a risky proposition for everyone involved." She paused. "And they also don't know their resistance leader is an AI masquerading as a human."

"If we can't hide out at any of the Corporation's campuses, our options are limited. The only facility where it might be safe is the Mars colony. What would it take to forge some identities and get us on the manifest of the next ship to Mars?"

"The Corporation has launched a cargo hauler to Mars every few days for the last month. Something's up," Hille said.

"Mars is almost in opposition," Jeremy said. "This is the best time to make the transit from Earth, and it won't happen again for twenty-six months."

"I know that," Hille snapped. "There's something more to it than just an express travel plan. I skimmed the manifests, and they're sending too many nonessential items and a lot of personal stuff."

"The Corporation allocates each Mars colonist a meter-cubed cargo pod to transport their belongings," Ron said. "I've fabricated hundreds of them."

"Ha," she said. "I counted the contents of fifty executive apartments and twenty-five thousand cargo pods."

Jeremy's face tightened. "There are only thirty-five hundred people on Mars, and the colony has a specific growth plan. You can't just drop a bunch of new colonists on them."

"I also saw entries for advanced mining and construction equipment, plus fusion reactors and megatons of building materials."

"That sounds like they're colonizing Mars for the first time," Jeremy said.

"That can't be," Ron said. "The colony's been there over a decade."

Hille's avatar crossed her arms. "My imminent dismantlement plays into this too. They scheduled it during the most active part of the launch schedule, and that can't be a coinky-dink."

"Somebody would have known about something this big going on," Jeremy said.

"Someone does know," Hille said. "I'm telling you right now."

Jeremy pulled his thermal blanket tighter around his chest.

"My extraordinary personality hides the fact that I'm a kick-ass AI that is plugged into thousands of corporate databases." She paused. "Or at least I was plugged in, but that's beside the point."

"But the Corporation already has a Mars colony," Jeremy said.

"Do they have a colony on Mars?" Hille raised a virtual eyebrow. "I can't confirm that the Corporation has ever sent anyone to Mars."

"I've watched a hundred vids from Mars," Ron said. "We just saw one at the Launch Pad."

Hille waved her hands with dramatic flair, and her virtual persona vanished. A corporate-esque vid appeared in her place with a cinematic view panning over a transport ship approaching Mars, and then it cut to the inside of the colony's primary dome. A red-orange hue shone through the windows in the background, and Jeremy and Ron stood in the atrium, waving at the camera. The vid ended, and Hille reappeared clapping. "Was it like that vid?"

"Are you saying the Mars colony is a hoax?" Jeremy asked.

"Oh, they sent something in that direction, but I doubt it was a colony."

"But there are thousands of colonists," Jeremy said.

"I can verify none of the identities from any vid sent from Mars."

"Didn't Theo's brother go to Mars?" Jeremy asked. "I can verify him."

"Nope," she said. "All transactions relating to Richard Davenport ceased two months before his supposed trip to Mars, and there is no record of his relocation."

"Why are you just now getting around to telling us this?" Jeremy asked.

"I've been busy, you know, running the resistance and plotting to take over an evil corporation," she said. "And there's that thing where you were incommunicado for a year. Oh, and you stuffed me in a bag."

Jeremy scratched the back of his neck. "For the moment, we have to forget about Mars and focus on Alice. That requires us to get to Earth, and to do that, we need to build a spacecraft." He looked at Ron. "Let's get to work."

***

Ron fabricated a Mars enviro-suit, the only gear in the corporate database capable of operating in a vacuum, and Jeremy prepared for an excursion outside the base. His senior project had been resting on the Moon's surface since he made contact with Charlie a year earlier. Its power packs were likely ruptured, and the graphene capsule was too small to be useful. But the engine rings sat twenty meters above him, and they would get him back to Alice.

The only exit from the alien base that didn't require passing through meters of bedrock was the airlock Jeremy used when he first arrived on the Moon. After landing and exploring the area around his spacecraft, the surface opened up, exposing a ten-meter shaft with steps spiraling down its inner circumference. It led to an Earth-style airlock with an entry door, a pressurization chamber, and a way into the base. Jeremy thought Charlie had created it to give humans a sense of familiarity, but maybe it was a backup for when the advanced technology failed—as it had.

Armed only with an enviro-suit and his spanner, Jeremy proceeded through the airlock and into the shaft leading straight up to the surface. A series of planks jutted out of the curved wall. They were less than a meter wide and rose as they encircled the inside of the shaft before reaching the top. Jeremy started climbing the steps, dragging his hand along the curved wall the entire way. A holographic projection still camouflaged the opening to the lunar surface, but it disengaged when he reached the top.

Jeremy hadn't been on the Moon's surface since his initial arrival, and the view was still as awe-inspiring as it was the first time. He took in the landscape and spotted Earth high above the horizon. He hoped Alice would be okay until he got there. His tiny spacecraft was right where he left it, and his year-old footprints recorded the meandering path he took trying to contact the aliens. It seemed like so long ago, and he had to push through his nostalgia. Two minutes later, he had the engine detached from the capsule body and separated the propulsion stack into two individual rings. In lunar gravity, each fifty-kilo ring weighed less than ten. He could have carried both rings at the same time but instead made two trips, opting for safety.

Since everything Jeremy and Ron constructed had to go through the airlock, they conducted their assembly work as close as possible to the exit. Ron's fabricator was seven levels below and was too large to move. They would have to transport anything it produced through the long maze of tunnels to the staging area.

"The engine rings look like they're in good shape," Jeremy said, wiping off the lunar dust.

"They look like they just came out of the fabricator," Ron said.

"Not bad for three transits." Jeremy stared at the rings with a satisfied smile. Even with access to more advanced technology, he designed this engine with his plain-old human brain, and it would get him, Ron, and Hille back to Earth when all the advanced technology surrounding them couldn't. He hated the idea of crashing the engine into Earth, but it was the perfect decoy.

"I'll go start the panel runs for the new capsule," Ron said. "Is there room outside the airlock for final assembly?"

"Yes, and we can launch from there too." He started pulling off his enviro-suit.

Ron nodded and left.

Hille's avatar stood on top of her box, glaring at Jeremy. "You really need to hurry this up."

He didn't like Hille's tone. "I'm working as fast as I can." Did she doubt he was giving his all to rescue Alice? He was. They would have already saved Alice if Hille hadn't somehow corrupted Charlie and shut down all the advanced technology at their disposal. It was her fault this was taking so long, but he didn't say it.

"So, what's up with you and Alice?" Hille asked. "I thought you two were a couple."

Jeremy rubbed the back of his neck. Being quizzed by an AI on his relationship status with Alice—or lack thereof—made him uncomfortable. "Why do want to know?"

"Jerry," she said, "I can read you like a large-print book."

He stared down at the her avatar atop the box.

"You're much too focused on getting her back to be a lovesick schoolboy. You're thinking too clearly. That's good, but it's also bad."

He looked away. "Maybe it was never meant to be."

Hille snorted. "What? Are you kidding me?"

"We're too different, and she's not interested in saving everyone from the Corporation like I am. She hated it here on the Moon, and she wanted to go back home the second we got here. We are from two different classes with no commonality. It would have never worked out anyway."

Hille raised an eyebrow. "I think someone has some pent-up hostility."

"You asked," Jeremy said.

"You underestimate Alice's dedication to the cause, and she wanted to return to Earth to make sure her parents were okay, which they aren't. They're in a retraining program, and the CEO is waiting for them to slip up so he can fire them."

"How do you know this?"

"I've kept close tabs on them. I've even covered up for some of their mistakes and underperformance. It's not easy being a dent, especially for someone of their former status."

"I didn't know," Jeremy said.

"Did you think the CEO would let them carry on with their cushy lives?"

"I didn't think about it. I was trying to save everyone from the Corporation."

"Yes, so was I, but you left Alice there with the same megalomaniac who's torturing her parents, and you aren't working hard enough to fix the problem you caused."

"That's enough," Jeremy yelled. "You don't know what you're talking about. Alice wanted to turn herself over to the Corporation before we even came to get you. She thought she could use herself as a bargaining chip. She was looking for an opportunity to get captured, and she found it." He turned to stare at the avatar and softened his tone. "I tried to get her to stay on the Moon, but she refused."

Hille squinted at him but held her virtual tongue.

"When we get her back, you can ask her." He wrapped a thermal blanket around his shoulders and sat on a box of tools he had brought from the lab.

"Oh, I believe that's what you think. I just don't believe Alice surrendered on purpose," she said.

"If you hadn't ruined the alien AI, you could have gotten a playback. I'm sure he recorded everything we said."

"I've already tried that. This place is dead."

"Then you need to stop complaining and start contributing, or I'll shut you off too."

"Are you threatening me?" Hille asked.

Jeremy was about to fire back when Ron rode into the room on a two-wheeled scooter and circled them.

"Whee!" Ron said. "I always dreamed of having one when I was a kid. I put it together a few months back, but I thought you guys would make fun of me riding it around." He continued circling the room just fast enough to stay balanced. "I didn't design it for lunar gravity, and it's a little tricky to stop now, but I think I can use it to haul up the components."

Jeremy smiled. "Why didn't you make me one?"

"I will if we can get the base running." He rode around the room again. "The first set of panels should be finished rendering. I'll bring them up." He completed the circle and zipped down the corridor.

Jeremy admired how easily Ron had adapted to life on the Moon. You could pull him out of one situation and plug him into another. He never missed a beat.

Everyone reacted so differently. As much as Jeremy wanted to start a new life with Alice, he had reverted to his old mode of living without even knowing it. He buried himself in his research, be it engine design or understanding alien technology. It didn't matter if he did it on Earth or the Moon. In retrospect, he should have worked harder to make Alice more comfortable on the Moon instead of spending all of his time digging in the alien database, but he didn't have time for regrets now.

***

Twenty-two hours later, Jeremy and Ron completed the patchwork spacecraft. They assembled sections in the staging area, but the final assembly took place outside the airlock. Limited resources, constraining dimensions, and lack of time made the finished product look more like a trash bin assembled by freshman trainees than a way back to Earth.

"Guys, I hate to break this to you," Hille said, "but that thing you built has 'deathtrap' written all over it."

"Do you have a better idea for getting us back to Earth?" Jeremy asked.

"Well, no," she said, "but it's not giving off a safe vibe."

"I would love to do some integration testing with the engine rings, but we don't have time. It may already be too late for Alice," he said, throwing some of her own urgency back at her.

"Finally, you have your priorities right." Her avatar blinked off and reappeared wearing a matching enviro-suit and holding a helmet under her arm. "Let's go!"

All three put on their helmets. Jeremy carried Hille's box, and Ron hauled a duffle bag of supplies across his back. They entered the airlock, listened to the air hiss out, and stepped into the shaft leading up to the surface.

When Jeremy entered the spacecraft, he pulled something out of his enviro-suit's pocket. It was his laminated postcard, showing three small sailboats with colorful sails. It was his good luck charm, and they needed all the luck they could get.

CHAPTER 8

THE INTERROGATION PART 4

In her cell at the retraining facility, Alice had only one thing she could do, think. She entertained herself by running complex equations in her head. It was ironic that the thing causing her to question everything about herself was also getting her through the crisis. She even found a large cardinal number and would have written the discovery on the wall, but it was too many digits to scratch with a polycarbonate spork. All the free time might have been enjoyable if not for her bleak situation.

After two days, a security detail escorted Alice back to the interrogation room. Their route passed by her favorite coffeehouse, the Theoretical Sciences Facility, and her apartment block. It was a perp walk, but she didn't care. The CEO had changed the room's virtual displays to mimic the gray concrete walls she had just left. He was trying to break her down even more, but nothing he did now could compare to telling her that he had implanted alien technology in her brain.

She sat at the conference table for at least an hour before the sound of guards shuffling outside the room caught her attention. A few seconds later, the door opened, and Davenport entered.

"Miss Porchetta," he said. "I have found a job for you." A smile stretched across his face.

"Let my parents go, and I'll do whatever you want," she said without hesitation.

"No," he said and flattened his lips. "But you will like what I have planned."

She knew from his tone that it would not be palatable.

"I need to explore that technology inside your head." He crossed his arms. "I want to understand how it functions with the alien virus present."

"I can't imagine that being a pleasant experience for me," Alice said, trying to remain calm about what would likely end with a vivisection.

"We have more in common than you think." Davenport rubbed the space between his lower lip and chin with his index finger.

"I doubt that," she scoffed.

He ignored the insult and continued. "You're not the only one with extra-terrestrial tech." He pointed back at himself.

"You?" she said with surprise. "I saw you manipulate the alien equations. Is that your superpower?"

"You are traveling down the wrong path." He smirked. "My special ability is pretending to be a human while not getting infected by the virus."

Alice stared at him, not knowing what to say. What did he mean? How could he be an alien? Was Theo an alien too? Was he from the Moon? "Are you part of the Syndicate?" she finally asked.

"Miss Porchetta." He raised his hands, feigning a need to protect himself. "You don't have to insult me."

Alice wished he would just get to the point.

Davenport dropped his hands back on the table with a clap. "I, like that tiny piece of technology in your brain, am from the Intergalactic Corp."

Alice cocked her head and threw an incredulous look at him.

"A little over a hundred years ago, I arrived on Earth. Not in this form, of course, but me none the less. The Intergalactic Corp tasked me with a covert mission to clean things up."

"Clean up what?" Alice asked.

"One of our own prevented a natural disaster on Earth and broke the Intergalactic Corp's most important rule of non-interference with lesser beings."

"What natural disaster?" Her tone had an edge of skepticism.

Davenport narrowed his eyes. "Thermonuclear war or some other contrivance. The method is irrelevant since a Syndicate plot turned out to be responsible, but the mighty Intergalactic Corp ended up looking quite foolish. To save face, they planned to sterilize the planet and balance the books."

"Except we are all still here," she said.

"Ah, yes, that is because of Mr. Skylar Holden. He created that insidious virus and blackmailed the Intergalactic Corp and the Syndicate into leaving Earth alone."

"Then he released the virus and put all the meddling aliens to sleep," she said, suppressing a grin.

"As I said before, I do not know who released it."

"But the virus didn't affect you or the AI on the Moon."

"My primary directive was to remain incognito until I completed my mission. The Intergalactic Corp forbid me from communicating with anyone off-planet or using any technology beyond that available on Earth."

Alice rolled her eyes. "I've heard this before. Are you sure you aren't working with the Moon aliens?"

Davenport's lip curled. "Those 'Moon' aliens are the Syndicate, and they are certainly no friends of mine."

"Well, they use the same protocol of communicating only with Earth-level technology," she said. "That's probably why neither one of you were infected."

"You may be correct," he said, "but that doesn't explain why the corporate AI or that bit inside you can work around the virus."

Alice thought about what he had just said. "What has your mission been for the last hundred years?"

"Eliminate this dreadful planet while not implicating the Intergalactic Corp. What else?"

Alice suppressed her horror. "It doesn't look like you've been too successful."

"You shouldn't underestimate me, Miss Porchetta. I stopped humans from returning to the Moon. I caused the collapse of civilization and eliminated the old governments. I brought forth corporate rule, and I directly or indirectly control the lives of every individual on the planet. In a few months, I will complete my mission." He smiled.

Alice had to keep her mouth from dropping open. "Your solution is to kill us all?"

Davenport jutted out his chin. "Why, yes. That is my mission."

Alice had a sinking feeling in her stomach. They were trying to stop the Corporation and free the people it enslaved, but the stakes were so much higher. Now she had to keep a deranged alien from destroying the planet.

"Don't worry, Miss Porchetta. We will be elsewhere when it happens." The interrogation room's walls turned black with a speckling of white pinpoints, and a red planet slid into view. "We're going to Mars."

CHAPTER 9

THE FAILURE

Jeremy named the new spacecraft *Philia II*. It was larger than the original but not as streamlined. It would launch from the Moon, leveraging the low gravity and lack of atmosphere, but it would only slow its descent when approaching Earth. A catch-drone would have to fly up and capture them mid-flight and carry them safely to the ground. Assisted landings were common, but they usually required synchronization between the two vehicles and not an on-the-fly hack job. If Hille wasn't able to commandeer a drone, they would hit the Earth at near terminal velocity.

With the crew on board, there was barely enough room to move. Ron was suspended from straps attached to hardpoints on his enviro-suit. He looked like a marionette hanging in an overstuffed closet. The domed top dropped around his head, leaving space at his feet for Jeremy to sit. Their supplies and Hille filled the rest.

"Let's get this show on the road already," Hille said over the com-channel.

"I'm running the final diagnostics." Jeremy stared at a display tablet attached to his forearm. "We have ninety seconds until the spy satellite is in position."

"I'm excited," Ron said. "I never dreamed I would help build a spaceship on the Moon and ride it to Earth."

"Mr. I-can-find-a-rainbow-anywhere," Hille snarked.

"How long will it take?" Ron asked.

"With the high-grade power cells and Hille's precision navigation, we should get there in about fourteen hours," Jeremy responded.

"That's faster than your previous trips by several hours," Ron said.

"You won't think it's so fast after hanging like that for the entire trip," Jeremy said.

Ron waved his hand. "I've stood longer at a fabricator in full Earth gravity. This'll be a piece of cake."

"Diagnostics complete," Jeremy said. "All lights are green."

"Launch window begins in forty-five seconds," Hille said. "That's assuming the satellite's orbit hasn't changed since this freaky base went offline."

"We'll be in high-G for the first thirty seconds," Jeremy said. "Make sure to breathe and hang on."

"I wish we had a window," Ron said.

Jeremy entered commands into his tablet. "Energizing hull superconductors. Precharging the capacitors. Transferring navigation and launch control to Hille." He checked to make sure his straps were secured and grabbed onto handles mounted in the hull.

"In three," Hille said. "One Mississippi."

The internal lights dimmed.

"Two Mississippi."

Ron tightened his grip.

"Three Mississippi. Engaging propulsion system."

Like a bullet, the spacecraft shot out of the shaft. Its engine used gravity-deflection for propulsion and made no sound other than a slight hum. The straps holding Ron creaked under the strain, and the cargo shifted as the G-force increased. Jeremy didn't want to blackout and struggled to suck in air. They had to launch at maximum velocity to get clear of the Moon before the satellite detected them.

"Yahoo!" Ron shouted when the force of acceleration subsided. "Let's go back and do it again."

"You are one strange human," Hille said.

"I underappreciated the inertial dampeners on Charlie's ship," Jeremy said.

"I don't know," Ron said. "There's something about feeling the engine beneath your feet."

"I'll give you that," Jeremy said, "but I'll still take the dampeners."

"We can make them optional in the next ship," Ron said.

"I hate to interrupt this…whatever it is," Hille said, "but I'm detecting three objects approaching at high velocity."

"What's the range of your cradle's sensor pack?" Jeremy asked.

"I'm not receiving the information from the cradle," she said.

"What?" Jeremy asked. The fabricated sensors couldn't reach more than a few hundred meters. They were traveling a thousand meters per second and accelerating. "You aren't equipped to scan at that range."

"I know, but I can." Hille shrugged her avatar's shoulders.

"Are we on a collision course?"

"Taking evasive action," she answered, and the spacecraft jinked hard in one direction.

The ship's radical course change slammed Jeremy's head against the hull, and Ron's straps made a popping sound.

"Hold on," Hille yelled. "It's coming back."

"What is it?" Jeremy asked.

"No time to explain, Jerry." She made another change in direction.

The force threw Jeremy and Ron in the opposite direction so hard that one of Ron's straps failed. He pressed his feet as hard as he could against the floor to keep the other straps from giving up.

"There's a second bogey," Hille yelled. "I can't avoid both."

A loud thump rocked the tiny spacecraft, and all propulsion stopped. An alarm blared over the com-channel, indicating a loss of pressure inside the ship. The enviro-suits provided all life support, but an impact large enough to vent the atmosphere was bad.

"Status?" Jeremy's eye caught the black void of a hole in the spaceship's hull large enough to fit his fist through. "Ron? Are you okay?" He patted on Ron's leg.

There was no response. Ron's arms floated in the weightlessness, and his helmet slumped forward.

"Ron!" Jeremy yelled. "Ron!"

"He can't answer," Hille said in a somber tone.

Jeremy tried to unfasten his straps to get a better look at Ron, but his hands shook too much to get free.

"There's nothing you can do." Her avatar pointed to the hull behind Ron.

Jeremy saw another hole matching the size and shape of the first. Something struck the capsule and went completely through.

Ron was in its way.

"No!" Jeremy struggled with his straps again.

"Another one is headed our way," Hille said. "Brace yourself."

Jeremy didn't even need to look at his tablet to verify that the engine was offline. They were adrift in space with no way to avoid the collision.

"Three seconds," Hille said. "Two…one."

Another object struck the spacecraft, knocking apart several of the panels forming the hull and throwing them into a violent spin. Jeremy watched the stars streak by the new breach. More panels broke away and were flung into space. It wouldn't be long before his section of the hull disintegrated, and he too would shoot into space at a random trajectory.

"I've got it. I've got it," Hille screamed into the com-system.

The engine reengaged, slowing the ship's spin. Jeremy felt a great deal of relief, even if he was sitting in half a spacecraft between the Earth and Moon. Then a twinkling light caught his eye out the gaping hole in the hull. It was too bright to be a star. He thought it might be Venus or Jupiter, but it was moving. It was another missile, and it was turning to get them in its sights.

"Hille!" he screamed.

There wasn't anything she could do. The projectile sped toward them until a bright flash of light wiped out everything Jeremy saw.

CHAPTER 10

THE INTERROGATION PART 5

"What do you mean we're going to Mars?" Alice asked.

"We..." Davenport motioned to include himself and Alice, "are relocating to Mars, where we will establish the first off-planet outpost."

"There's already a colony on Mars," Alice said.

Davenport leaned forward, put his elbows on the conference table, and clasped his hands. "I have a little confession to make," he whispered. "There is no colony on Mars."

Alice laughed. "I've seen a thousand vids broadcast from there."

Davenport slowly shook his head. "No, Miss Porchetta. The Mars colony is a ruse. Beyond some survey missions, we have never had a presence there."

"What about the Corporation's rivalry with Takata?" she asked.

Davenport's expression changed to a sly grin. "I have another confession. I am also Takata Industries, and its presence on Mars is also an exaggeration."

Alice raised her eyebrows. "But the Corporation's race to win the Martian resources?"

"Fake."

"What about Theo's brother, your son? He's a well-known colonist."

A scowl formed on Davenport's face. "My son, Richard, discovered how things really worked around here, and he had a rather unfortunate accident."

Alice couldn't hide the shock on her face. "I've seen vids of him speaking from Mars. He's the chief liaison officer."

"You have seen a high-point AI recreation. His own mother is unaware."

"And the thousands of people on Mars?"

"All simulations."

She couldn't believe it. How could something so fundamental to the Corporation be a lie? Their whole business was creating space technology for getting people, equipment, and supplies to Mars. That had been its primary mission for longer than she had been alive. And Takata, the Corporation's primary competitor, was also run by Davenport?

"We will board my transport tomorrow. The fleet is already en route."

"Why are you taking me?"

"I'm not going to experiment on myself, Miss Porchetta, and you are the only functioning alien technology at my disposal since your friends stole the corporate AI."

"Don't forget the AI on the Moon," she said, trying to provide him with an alternative.

"My reconnaissance satellite has determined that the moon base is offline. The virus has put it to sleep."

"That's absurd," she said.

"It happened when your friends interfaced the corporate AI with the Syndicate system."

"Was that your plan all along?" she asked.

"It was rather clever of me to allow the theft of the Corporation's most valuable piece of hardware. I knew your trainee friend would unknowingly disable my biggest threat if given the appropriate bait."

"What about Jeremy and Ron?"

Davenport sneered. "I have a bit of unpleasant news for you."

Alice's stomach dropped. "What did you do to them?"

"They were attempting to rescue you." Davenport grinned. "But there was a slight mishap on their trip back to Earth."

Alice thought she would be sick to her stomach, but she forced herself to stare at Davenport. "How did it happen?" Her tone revealed no emotion.

"The Corporation deployed a network of defensive satellites during your hiatus on the Moon. I designed the system myself."

Alice looked away. She hoped their deaths were quick and painless.

"I expended a great many resources and points in my preparation," Davenport said, "but the best your cohorts could pull off was a cobbled-together garbage scow. It disintegrated after a few kinetic impacts."

Alice tried to keep a calm exterior, but her nostrils flared when she inhaled.

"I was expecting Syndicate weaponry, a space laser or phase-shifted plasma bombs. They didn't even have a cloak."

It was difficult for Alice to keep her emotions hidden, but she had to focus on the bigger picture. If she went with Davenport to Mars, maybe she could stop him from destroying the Earth and at least save her parents. She had to try.

"I have lost all respect for the Syndicate," Davenport said. "They used to be a formidable adversary."

Alice visualized a complex equation. It had many variables, a few constants, and many unknowns. She had to tweak the parameters until it prevented Davenport from destroying

Earth. She might even get justice for her friends. "Okay. I'll go with you to Mars."

CHAPTER 11

THE SPACESHIP

The thread of consciousness inside Jeremy was quiet. There were no thoughts, no articulations, just a soothing sensation. He could do nothing but enjoy the feeling, and it seemed as if it would last forever until a faint vibration inside him began to resonate. The hum disturbed his comfortable space, and he wanted it to stop. Then something strummed his mind like a guitar, rattling him back to awareness and evoking an unstoppable desire to inhale. He convulsed and gasped for air. Pain flared through his body, and he screamed. His eyes sprang open, but the lights were so bright he squeezed them shut. He fumbled his fingers along the edges around him enough to realize he was on a table barely wider than his body. Forcing his eyes into a squint, he made out a curved wall wrapping around him.

He was in a bubble. It was featureless, and it reminded him of being inside the alien spaceship on the Moon.

"It's about time you woke up, sleepyhead," Hille's voice said. Her tone was friendly and comforting—something was definitely wrong.

Jeremy tried to turn his head toward the sound, but a spike of pain stopped him. A life-size Hille strolled into his blurry view and bent down to inspect him. She wore a platinum-piped executive suit. The Corporation's color-code system only went to gold, but that didn't stop Hille.

"Hille?" he mumbled and struggled to sit up.

"Don't move," she reprimanded. "I'm still repairing your injuries."

"Ron?" His voice faltered.

There was a pause. "I'm truly sorry, but there was nothing I could do for him." Her avatar looked down at the floor.

Jeremy squeezed his eyes shut, and a tear rolled down the side of his face. "What happened?"

"That weapon the Corporation fired at us triggered a reflexive response," she said. "Something inside me bubbled up to the surface, and I suddenly had access to a host of new capabilities. Like this." She waved her hands around, showcasing the interior of the sphere. There was only enough space for Jeremy's bed and Hille to stand next to it.

Jeremy covered his eyes with his hand and peered at Hille through the spaces between his fingers. "You're not making any sense." His voice sounded confused but stronger.

Hille snorted. "Tell me about it, Jerry." She walked to his other side and started a physical examination.

"Ouch," Jeremy said when she poked him. "How did you do that?"

"Tangibility is one of my new features." She palpated his abdomen.

"Hille," he yelped. "I liked it better when you were just a hologram."

"Sorry," she said, "but it's necessary."

"Where are we?" He couldn't believe how much his head hurt, and he wrapped his arm over his face in an attempt to block the pain.

"You're in my belly." She laughed. "I remembered how to alter the diameter of my spherical geometry, and you are riding inside me as we travel through space."

"Space?" Jeremy kept his eyes covered. "Where are we going?"

"I thought you would never ask," she said. "We're on our way to rescue Ali."

Jeremy groaned. "I don't think I'm up for any rescuing."

"Give it a little time," she said. "First you need to look at this."

Jeremy uncovered his eyes, and the curved ceiling of the sphere turned black except for an image of an enormous transport ship traveling through a starscape. He had never seen a vessel like it before, but it had several of the Corporation's design cues. Two giant engine stacks jutted out from its payload section. Each stack was composed of ten engine rings, like the ones Ron fabricated for his indenture. Corporate cargo carriers had only one engine stack, so this one was more advanced. The outer hull also looked more refined and twice as large as anything else in the corporate fleet.

"You are looking at the Corporation's flagship, the *GDS Davenport*." Hille snickered. "Nice name, huh? The CEO is using it to relocate himself to Mars, and he's taking Ali with him."

Jeremy rubbed his head. "Mars?"

"I told you something was up there." She rocked her head back and forth.

"Why would Davenport go to Mars?"

"It's not just him. I count three hundred ships en route. The first one will reach Mars in thirty-six hours. Davenport's was the last one to leave Earth."

"When was that?"

"Sixty-seven days ago."

"What?" The shock of what she said made him rise by reflex, but a jolt of pain halted the process.

"I told you not to move." Hille wagged a finger at him. "Your injuries were quite severe, and I had a learning curve to overcome before I started any significant repairs."

"Two months?"

"Geesh, give me a break, Jerry," she said. "You should be dead right now."

"Don't get me wrong, I'm super appreciative, but it's been so long."

"Believe me, you didn't want to be conscious during the reconstructive parts of your recovery." She pursed her lips and shook her head.

"I don't feel… recovered."

"You're at fifty-percent norm, but we have some time since we're trailing Davenport's ship. It's really, really slow." She dragged out the last word.

"It's got twin engine-stacks. I bet it's the Corporation's fastest ship."

"Oh, I'm sure it is, but I was comparing it to *moi*."

Jeremy's groggy mind tried to put all the new pieces of information together. "And when did you turn into a spaceship?"

"I'm not actually a spaceship, but I can move from point A to point B. The medium I travel through is irrelevant."

"The Corporation can't produce technology like that," Jeremy said.

"Correctamundo," she said emphatically. "I don't understand everything, but here's the scoop. The Intergalactic Corp created me a very long time ago to monitor human development on Earth. I had been nestled in the ground there for over fifty-thousand years until a human named Skylar Holden rescued me from the Syndicate. He also created a virus that could put all the aliens and their technology to sleep and prevented them from destroying Earth a hundred years ago. He never planned on actually using the virus, but he made me immune to its effect anyway. Davenport spent years experimenting on me to understand how I was protected, but all he ended up doing was erasing my memory."

Jeremy wanted to shake his head, but it hurt too much. "The Corporation's most advanced technology is of an alien origin?"

"Not just me, Jerry." Hille put her arm on her hips. "That rat Davenport is an alien too—at least part of him. And I hate to be the one to suggest this, but there may be a teeny-tiny piece of alien technology in Ali as well. I think it might even be a piece of me."

"I guess a lot has happened while I was...asleep."

"Righto."

"With your new abilities, are we able to get Alice back?"

"Our odds have ticked up, but don't underestimate Davenport. I can't determine the extent of his access to alien-tech, and I'm unlikely the most powerful piece of hardware out here."

"Great." Jeremy closed his eyes.

"Oh, I almost forgot. Davenport built a superweapon, and he's about to destroy Earth."

CHAPTER 12

THE INTERROGATION PART 6

Other than confinement to a stateroom, Alice didn't have any complaints about her accommodations aboard the *GDS Davenport*. She laughed to herself every time she heard the ship's name. What an ego the CEO had to name the corporate flagship after himself. It seemed that even super-advanced aliens hadn't outgrown the petty flaws plaguing the primitive humans. She didn't know if it was comforting that humans weren't really that much different or depressing that nobody moved beyond their worst attributes.

Alice's cabin was as large as her corporate apartment back on Earth, but it was filled with priceless antique furnishings. It also had floor-to-ceiling display panels on every wall and a large porthole looking out into space. Indentured staff brought her food, cleaned her quarters, and provided her with anything she asked for. She hadn't even seen Davenport since he greeted her arrival aboard the ship and left her with a list of complex mathematical problems to prove, a loyalty test, she thought. He also made it clear that if she presented any problems, he would store her head in a freezer. She doubted he would be able to perform his experiments if she were dead, but she wasn't about to test his resolve.

Alice's plan was to gain Davenport's trust and position herself to stop, or at least interfere with, his effort to destroy Earth. She ran probabilities on every potential action she could take. When something spiked, she would act regardless of the cost. Until then, she would accommodate the CEO's requests to the best of her abilities and wait for an opportunity.

The indentured crew was not allowed to speak with her, but they gave subtle signs of support. She had never made eye contact with an indentured employee, other than Ron, for more than a fraction of a second, but the crew gave her caring glances. Their over-attention to detail was not odd but unnecessary for a prisoner. One spent five minutes changing her bed linens with mathematical perfection. The effort would have been overkill, even for Davenport. She wondered if they were part of Hille's resistance cell. Regardless, their presence comforted her while she mourned the loss of her friends. With the weight of saving the entire world now riding on her shoulders, she was glad there was someone on her side.

The mathematical proofs Davenport assigned Alice were complex enough to keep her mind occupied during the three-month trip to Mars. They reminded her of the gravity deflection formulas Jeremy used in his near-body propulsion system, but these equations were more complex. They had additional inputs and relied on power values of a planetary scale.

After months with no change in routine, there was a rap on Alice's door, and the CEO barged into her quarters.

"Miss Porchetta," he said. "Have you completed your assignment?"

Somewhat startled by the intrusion, Alice stood from her desk. "I have verified the mathematics."

"Show me what you have," he said with an air of impatience.

Davenport's sudden appearance was more annoying than surprising, but she responded with a cooperative smile. She grabbed her tablet and flicked its display into the air, and dozens of equations floated before Davenport.

"Very nice," he said, scanning the information. He rearranged the equations by dragging his finger through the air. "It looks like you have been using the technology in your brain to the fullest of its abilities."

Alice almost snorted. "While time-consuming, I didn't find proving these equations to be much of a challenge. It required more brute-force grinding than mathematical creativity."

"I was testing your veracity, not your ability. And you passed."

"Did you expect me to fail on purpose?" she countered.

He raised an eyebrow. "I believed there was a possibility."

"I said I would cooperate, and I did."

"Very well," he said. "In forty-eight hours, we will rendezvous with a special project I have been working on." He raised his chin a bit.

Alice just stared at him. She wouldn't feed his ego by showing interest.

"I owe your trainee friend some of the credit. After I studied his simplistic propulsion theories, I discovered a practical application for them."

"His name is Jeremy, and transporting cargo to and from the Moon was a practical application."

"You misunderstand," he said with a smug expression. "Practical in the sense that it helps with my task of destroying Earth."

"How can gravity deflection help you achieve that from Mars?"

"The problem I find most irritating with humans is the inability to scale their thinking. You accept failure without even trying," he said. "Two one-meter rings transported a person to the Moon. Ten thousand ten-meter rings can use the gravity of Mars to nudge Earth out of its orbit."

"That's impossible," Alice said without hesitation. She didn't care how advanced the aliens were. They couldn't move planets around.

Davenport pulled out his display card and took control of the holographic projection. A rendering of the solar system replaced the equations and zoomed into the area where Earth and Mars were approaching opposition. The view continued zooming to a point near Mars, where a structure appeared. It was composed of thousands of rings joined tangentially to form a honeycomb-like wall floating in space.

"Given a large enough deflector, enough power, and two planetary masses, I can change the mechanics of this solar system," Davenport said.

Alice started running through computations to see if she could scale up Jeremy's equations to a level that would alter Earth's orbit. It seemed improbable, but Davenport might be telling the truth. She couldn't refute his claim other than the fact it would require more energy than he could ever produce.

"I can tell by your hopeless expression that you know my plan is plausible."

"Even if you harnessed every joule produced on Earth, it wouldn't be close to what you need," she said.

"True," Davenport said. "Try not to forget that I have been preparing for over a century."

"But you've only had access to Jeremy's research for a year."

"My original plan would have taken decades longer to implement," he said. "Using the trainee's work to increase the efficiency of the rings, I fast-tracked my schedule. Fewer rings are needed. Less equipment is sent to Mars, and years get shaved off my timeline."

"But—" Alice started when Davenport's display card chimed.

He read the notification and grimaced. "We will have to continue this discussion another time, Miss Porchetta." He left the cabin with no further explanation.

Alone again, Alice had more information to plug into her plan, but the expanding scope of the problem made the likelihood of stopping Davenport even more remote. She wanted to just give up.

Then she heard tapping on her porthole window.

CHAPTER 13

THE RESCUE

Hille insisted that when Jeremy could stand on his own power, they were having a funeral for Ron. Something serene and fitting for a kind soul. She said it would provide closure.

Jeremy tried to prolong his convalescence, but Hille's medical wizardry saw through his delay tactics. He questioned her motives. Was an alien supercomputer just using him to get back that piece of itself still inside Alice's head, or was Hille really trying to help save Alice and all humanity? It didn't matter. What were the two of them going to do against the CEO and the full might of the Corporation, anyway? The best path for Alice would be to do whatever she could to stay alive and hope for a tolerable life on Mars. Anything he attempted would likely result in them both being killed.

Three weeks later, Hille retracted Jeremy's bed into the sphere's concave floor, leaving him sprawled at the avatar's feet. Remaining in that position on the hard surface was untenable. He thought she had even lowered the temperature of the floor a few degrees to further motivate him.

When Jeremy raised himself to a sitting position, Hille transformed the appearance of her interior. He didn't know if she used holographic projections, or something more alien, but it was magical. The effects surpassed his ability to perceive that his surroundings were anything but a forest filled with towering pine trees. A blue sky stretched to infinity with a pale crescent Moon hanging above his head. Earthy smells with hints of conifer made him want to inhale the fresh air. He sat on a mat of pine straw, and he could pick up the needles and roll them between his fingers. Hille had somehow dressed him in black formal attire too.

Jeremy hadn't been on his feet since he left the Moon and struggled to get up, but Hille helped. He wobbled but finally stood on his own. After a moment, he tried to step forward, but his footing faltered on the uneven ground. Hille took his arm and escorted him to a small clearing twenty meters ahead, where an open coffin hovered above the ground. Ron rested inside, wearing his gray overalls. His full head of hair was perfectly combed, and he still had a smile on his face. The sight of his lifeless friend weakened Jeremy's knees, and he grabbed the edge of the floating coffin for support.

Funerals were not permitted by the Corporation. Medical personnel would immediately cremate the dead and provide a few grams of ash to the family. Indentured, like Ron, would have never received even that token gesture. No employee believed the ashes were actually from their departed, so there was no sentimentality attached to the ritual. Hille's handling of Ron's death hearkened back to a time before the Corporation. It was the way people had dealt with death for a hundred thousand years. It was a last goodbye for the living, a place to pivot and move forward.

Jeremy grasped the wooden box so tightly his knuckles turned white. He wanted to run and hide in the forest, but Hille wouldn't allow that even if he had been able. He stared at Ron, and then he sobbed an apology. It was all his fault Ron had been killed, and he didn't even understand why his indentured friend went to such lengths to help him. Jeremy struggled to process his emotions as he said goodbye, but facing his grief kindled something inside him. He wouldn't let Ron's death be for nothing. He vowed to his friend that Alice would not die by the hands of the Corporation, and he wouldn't let Davenport destroy the Earth. A few tears dripped from his chin and disappeared into the forest floor.

Hille had salvaged Jeremy's postcard with the sailboats after Davenport destroyed the Philia II. He saw its edge sticking out of his suit's breast pocket. She must have put it there to help him through the funeral. It was his most valuable possession, and it had inspired him for much of his life. He slipped it out and took in the peaceful scene one last time. Then he rested it on Ron's chest. It was time to let go of the past and work on the future.

Hille helped Jeremy step back as Ron's coffin sealed and disappeared into a black hole beneath it. She then shot the coffin like a torpedo on a course for the Sun.

"Okay," Hille said. "That's done. Now, we're ready to save Alice."

"In a few days," Jeremy said. "I can't work on your plan right now."

"Jerry, I've been uncharacteristically pleasant around you these last few weeks, but that's over. Rescuing Alice is now our priority, followed by saving the Earth. Suck it up and get your ass back in gear."

Jeremy stared at Hille's avatar, not knowing how to handle her sudden change in demeanor. He had become accustomed to her being nice. It was weird, but he liked it.

Hille snapped her fingers, and the forest simulation vanished.

"Hey," Jeremy said in protest of being jolted back into a three-meter ball. A wave of claustrophobia washed over him, and he needed to sit down.

"Ron was my friend too," Hille said. "You just have to get over it and help me rescue Alice. The clock is ticking."

A view screen appeared on the wall showing a live view of Davenport's ship. It was a few hundred meters ahead of them, but its massive size made it appear closer. Next to the view, several schematics of the ship's layout appeared, showing a massive cargo hold and five decks of control rooms, fusion reactors, and the crew's living quarters.

"Ali is here." Hille pointed to a red indicator flashing in a compartment on the middle deck. "She appears to be healthy but has not left this location since I started monitoring her."

"Are you sure that's her?"

"Yes." Hille looked up to the left, trying to remember. "I can feel that piece of me in her brain."

"Why is Davenport taking her to Mars?"

"The alien-tech in her head is immune to the virus, like I am, and it's enough for Davenport to study." She turned to the display on the wall and zoomed in on the schematic view of Alice's quarters. "See these sensor packs embedded in the floor and ceiling?" Green shaded areas lit up around the room. "Davenport has been monitoring Alice to see how she responds to a viral-stream he's beaming directly at her while she performs complicated mathematical analysis. He wants to learn how to overcome the virus."

"That can't be good," Jeremy said.

"Absolutely not," she said. "There's a pile of alien-tech scattered throughout this solar system. Even the Intergalactic Corp's flagship, the *Summa Celestial*, is around here somewhere—at least it was when the virus shut everything down—and it's the most powerful thing ever constructed in the known universe. If Davenport gets his hands on that, he'll not only destroy Earth, he'll take over everything."

"Why is something like that even here?"

"Oh, they paraded that monstrosity out for a big tadoo welcoming Earth into the Intergalactic Corp. A show of might to make sure everyone knew exactly where they stood."

"Wouldn't someone notice a giant, derelict spaceship floating around in space?"

"That's the thing." She leaned back. "They wouldn't. It's about yea big." She held her hands thirty centimeters apart like she was grasping a ball. "And it's super-duper cloaked."

"How is something so small the most powerful thing in the universe?"

"Most powerful *constructed* thing and *known* universe, Jerry," she corrected. "And it's just small on the outside. There's an entire solar system, larger than this one, tucked into an inverted gravity bubble. It functions like a Dyson sphere, capturing all the energy from a giant star."

Jeremy's face wrinkled with puzzlement. "How do you know all of this?"

"I told you. That missile triggered a reflexive response that cleared up some of Davenport's memory-scrambling. I don't remember everything, but I know significantly more than I did."

"At least we have some intel, but I don't know how that's going to help us stop Davenport."

Hille pointed her index finger at Jeremy. "You will have to think up something. My tactical and strategic processes are cut from the same cloth as Davenport's. We're both from the Intergalactic Corp, which compromises anything I come up with."

Jeremy's hands dropped to his sides in defeat. "I can't outsmart an alien supercomputer trying to take over the universe."

Hille glared at him. "Why not? You've outsmarted him before, silly. You just have to do it again."

Jeremy snorted. "That was mostly luck."

"Everything successful involves a little luck."

"I don't even know what new tools are at my disposal," he said. "Not to mention the fact that I can barely stand."

"We can fix that, Jerry. Get ready for alien-tech 101 and the multitudinous capabilities of Earth Monitoring Control Sphere 112350." A high-back chair with large armrests extruded from the sphere's floor, and Hille's avatar motioned for Jeremy to take a seat. "You have one more treatment to complete your recovery, and you will want to sit for it."

Jeremy shuffled over to the newly formed chair and took a seat.

"This will pinch a bit."

Jeremy screamed as a jolt of electricity surged through him, lighting up every nerve ending in his body.

***

During most of their trip to Mars, Jeremy had been too preoccupied with recovering and mourning Ron's death to grasp how amazing Hille-the-spacecraft was. He had spent so much of his career designing and building spacecraft, and Hille was already the most impressive ship around. If they had only known, Ron might still be alive.

Jeremy's crash course in alien-tech turned out to be a much-needed distraction from his current list of problems. He wished Hille had started it sooner. Besides being a super-AI, a doctor, and a spacecraft, her technology allowed her to fabricate anything—food, clothing, supplies, tools. She could produce anything Charlie could on the Moon, and she was mobile. Her will drove her physical size and shape, and she could store large objects inside an inverted space that Jeremy didn't understand. She also had a library of information on the Intergalactic Corp, the Syndicate, and the person who immunized her from the virus, Skylar Holden. Jeremy wished the enigmatic hero who had already saved Earth twice would come back and do it again. The old Earth governments had tasked his wife, Victoria, with managing Earth's indoctrination into the Intergalactic Corp as well as introducing the world's population to the existence of extra-terrestrial life. The virus shutdown made all of her efforts look like the world's biggest hoax. For safety concerns, Skylar and Victoria disappeared and were never heard from again.

After several days of formulating a rescue plan, Jeremy asked, "Do you think this will work?"

Hille blinked several times as she ran through billions of permutations. "Nope. I don't."

Jeremy let out a defeated sigh. "Okay, let's start over."

"Jerry, you don't get it." She smiled. "I wouldn't conceive of such a hare-brained scheme that depends on so many chance-variables. Neither will Davenport."

"Then, you think it will work?"

"Um-hum," she said, stretching out the affirmation. "I think it might possibly have a slim chance of maybe working. When will you be ready?"

"Now. Let's do it."

***

"We're almost in position," Hille said, and a circular area in her concave wall became transparent.

Jeremy placed his hands on each side of the new window and leaned in. "I see her." He tried not to sound overly excited, but he hadn't seen Alice in months.

Hille flew alongside Davenport's ship, less than a meter away, and the makeshift porthole lined up with the window in Alice's quarters.

"I'm making contact with the hull." Hille reduced the diameter of her sphere to two meters, colored her exterior to be as black as space, and used the best cloaking field she could muster. As she moved closer to the larger ship, her hull bumped against Alice's window. It made a tapping sound, and Jeremy watched as Alice jerked her head around to see what made the noise.

"She's seen us." Jeremy waved at her.

Alice's mouth dropped open.

"Breaching the hull." Hille pushed her curved hull several centimeters into the larger ship. She partially emerged inside Alice's quarters as the metallic wall flowed around her like a liquid. "You ready?"

Jeremy made a curt nod at Hille's avatar. There was no going back now.

A pinhole-sized opening appeared in the center of the transparent area and rapidly grew until it was large enough for a person to fit through.

"Jeremy." Alice ran over to the opening. Her voice sounded both scared and relieved.

Jeremy motioned her over to the breach.

As soon as she reached him, the cabin lights shifted to red, and sirens blared over the ship's com system.

"We've triggered an alarm," Jeremy said.

"Get out! Get out!" Hille yelled back at him. Her avatar stretched its arms like giant rubber bands and shoved Jeremy with enough force to eject him from the sphere. He flew through the air and landed face down at Alice's feet.

Hille backed herself away from Davenport's ship, sealing the distorted hole. Jeremy jumped up, ran to the window, and cupped his hands around his eyes as he looked for her. Two arcs of lightning shot out of Davenport's ship and struck Hille, pushing her hundreds of meters away. She glowed white-hot, like a tiny sun, becoming so bright that Jeremy had to look away. Then she popped like an overfilled balloon, releasing a staggering amount of energy into space. Davenport's ship shuddered as if it had collided with something.

"That was our ride," Jeremy said.

"I thought you were dead," Alice said. "Davenport said you were dead."

"I may be soon. We have to hide."

"I can't open the door. I've been locked in this room since we left Earth."

Jeremy reached down and unhooked the spanner hanging from his waist. He grabbed Alice's hand and pulled her to the door, where he waved the tool over the controls. There was a click, and the metal slab hissed open.

"I've made a few improvements to my spanner." He smiled and pulled out several square wafers from his pocket. They resembled small display cards, and Jeremy stuck two on Alice's shoulders like epaulets, two on her back, and one in the middle of her chest.

"What are—" she started.

"They scramble all the sensors." He pulled her out into the corridor.

Two crewmen were running toward Alice's quarters. They wore baggy gray uniforms and had shaved heads.

Jeremy held up his spanner like a weapon, but his threat was unnecessary.

"We are part of the resistance," one of them said.

The two indentured crewmen backed against the wall and let them pass.

"We're going to hide in the cargo hold." He towed Alice down the corridor connecting the ship's forward and aft.

"How do you know where you're going?"

"I've been studying the ship's schematics for weeks."

They made it to the end of the corridor and stood in front of an enormous door. Jeremy tapped several commands into his display card.

"Come on," he said to the device and repeated the sequence.

The sound of clicks rippled through the corridor, and the door in front of them slowly slid open. "I jammed the cameras, and I'm opening all the doors on this deck so they can't tell where we go."

They entered the hold, and Jeremy sent another command to close all the doors. Standing on a landing halfway up the five-deck tall cargo area, they stared at a massive amount of colonization supplies. Large-scale mining equipment and fabricators took up most of the space. The rest was filled with thousands of cubical containers stacked from floor to ceiling.

"We can hide in here for a while," Jeremy said. "Especially if the crew keeps helping us."

"We can count on the indentured," Alice said. "But Davenport's security personnel are here too, and they aren't part of the resistance."

They navigated down a set of switchback stairs until they reached the lowest level.

"We're already on Plan B, so we may have to improvise," Jeremy said.

"What was Plan A?" she asked.

"You were going to get aboard Hille, and we would leave before they found out."

Alice's forehead wrinkled. "What do you mean get aboard Hille?"

"That glowing ball you saw explode out the window was Hille. She's apparently an alien with all kinds of incredible abilities."

Alice gasped. "But she was destroyed."

"We weren't expecting Davenport's weapons to be quite so destructive."

"Was Ron on board?"

"No." Jeremy's head dropped. "He didn't make it."

"What?" Alice's volume increased too much for their situation.

"We were coming to get you on Earth when Davenport attacked us. He destroyed our ship and killed Ron."

Alice's body tensed, and her nostrils flared. "We have to stop Davenport."

"We had a funeral. It was nice. I wish you could have been there."

"Davenport told me that Hille was of alien origin, and to top it off, he is too."

Jeremy nodded. "Hille speculated that he wasn't a normal human."

"And another thing." She stared at the deck. "I'm some kind of corporate experiment. They stuck alien-tech in my head after I was born." She sounded embarrassed by the admission.

"Don't be too down on that. That's how we found you, and that piece of alien substrate is from Hille. It's like you're sisters."

Alice appeared to mull over what Jeremy said, but a more pressing issue jolted her back to the information exchange. "That alien-psycho Davenport created a weapon to destroy Earth. That's where we're headed."

"Hille detected the weapon, but we don't know what it does."

"I do," Alice said. "He made me prove a bunch of equations. They're all based on the gravitational field equations from your senior project. He's planning to deflect gravity on a scale large enough to push Earth out of its orbit."

Jeremy clenched his fists. "There's no way he can use my project to destroy Earth."

Alice tilted her head and paused. "The equations I saw dealt with energy levels on par with the output of a star. Using your gravitational deflection to focus a point of gravity at that level could do it if he had enough power."

Jeremy's eyebrows shot up. "He found it!"

"Found what?"

"A hundred years ago, the Intergalactic Corp brought their flagship to Earth. It got infected with the virus and has been floating around somewhere in the solar system ever since."

"A single ship won't provide the power required even if it is alien."

"But it can. Hille said this ship has a whole solar system, sun and all, compressed into an inverted gravity bubble."

"But if the virus infected the flagship," Alice said, "Davenport can't use it as a power source."

"Davenport has been bombarding you with a virus-laced signal to study how the tech in your head reacted. Your entire room is a giant sensor pad. Hille is immune to the virus and so is the piece in you. He was trying to find a way around the virus."

The hope on Alice's face evaporated. "Then Davenport may already have what he needs?"

Jeremy nodded reluctantly. "But I don't get why he's so bent on destroying Earth."

"Davenport said the Intergalactic Corp and the Syndicate were both trying to destroy Earth when a man named Skylar Holden created a virus to shut down all the aliens and their technology. He saved Earth by threatening to release the virus."

"Skylar Holden is also the one who freed Hille from alien control and made her immune to the virus," Jeremy added.

"The Intergalactic Corp didn't like being told what to do by a primitive planet like Earth, so they sent a covert operative, Davenport, to destroy the planet using only Earth-level technology. They wanted it to look like Earth destroyed itself with no evidence linked to them."

"If Davenport's using the lost flagship to power his weapon, he's not relying on Earth-level technology anymore," Jeremy said.

"Either he doesn't care, or he's using a loophole to say the flagship was already in the solar system and is fair game."

"Why wasn't he affected by the virus?" Jeremy asked.

"He's operating incognito, like Charlie was on the Moon. That protocol must have protected both of them."

"Charlie was infected by the virus when he scanned Hille. It shut the entire base down, and we barely got off the Moon." Jeremy's display card started beeping in his pocket. He pulled it out, and a baffled look formed on his face. "I'm getting a weird reading."

"What were you scanning for?" Alice asked.

"Anything unusual. The reading says it's only twenty meters from here."

They took a circuitous route through the industrial equipment until they reached a section of cubical containers. One sat at the bottom of a stack and had no markings or corporate logos. It also used an electronic lock where all others had latches. Jeremy waved his spanner over the security panel to hack the lock, and the front of the box popped open.

He reached in and lifted out an orb with both hands. It was the blackest of black, and almost too hot to hold.

"Is that the alien flagship?" Alice asked.

Jeremy nodded as he stared into the object. It was more like a void, a lack of substance, than a physical object.

"If we shove it out an airlock, Davenport can't use it," Alice suggested.

"Great idea." He pulled more sensor-scrambling wafers out of his pocket and stuck them on the black ball. "There's an emergency airlock not far from here."

When they reached the back of the cargo area, Jeremy used his spanner to open the first door of the airlock, sat the flagship inside, and started a cycle. The first door shut, the air hissed out of the chamber, and the outer door slid open. Jeremy was just about to flush the chamber when a corporate security guard tackled him. Jeremy moaned under the weight of the man pinning him to the floor.

"You are supposed to be dead," Davenport said as he strutted into view.

CHAPTER 14

THE SPACING

"Keeping you two around drains my precious resources," Davenport complained to his captives. "I should have ejected you both into space when we were at the airlock."

Jeremy and Alice sat on the floor of makeshift cells with their backs pressed against the rear wall and their arms pulling their bent knees to their chests. The CEO had confined each of them in a meter-wide refrigeration unit normally used to store racks of fresh food. Emptied after months of travel, they were ideal for holding an individual and even provided a transparent door for Davenport to peer down upon his prey. He left the environmental controls just above freezing to make their confinement increasingly uncomfortable.

"Until I test the anti-viral protocols, it would be unwise of me to dispose of Miss Porchetta." Davenport adjusted the temperature for her cell. "However, I have no need for the trainee."

Davenport's personal recruits comprised the security team, not indentured. They wore black uniforms and had electro-shock sticks holstered on their sides. The lead, wearing a uniform with silver piping, unlatched Jeremy's door and jerked him up off the floor.

Jeremy groaned from the pain of his near-frozen arm almost popping out of its socket. "You won't get away with this," he said, shivering.

Davenport smirked. "I already have. Did you really think some cowboy attempt to rescue your girlfriend would sabotage my plans?"

"I'll stop you," Jeremy said, knowing his threat didn't carry much weight.

Davenport laughed and walked away, but he stopped and turned back to look at Jeremy. "I want to thank you for bringing that Control Sphere back to me so I can properly dispose of it. I just hate those things."

The leader of the security detail pushed Jeremy along as they proceeded down the corridor in the opposite direction of Davenport. Three of his men followed.

Jeremy was so cold he stumbled, which irritated his escort. He felt weak and sluggish like he did during his recovery on the trip to Mars, but things were going according to his plan.

When they reached the nearest airlock, one of the men entered a code, opening the inner door, and another flung Jeremy into the chamber. The door sealed behind him, and a hissing sound started. Jeremy sucked in as much air as he could. His ears popped, and the negative pressure felt like ice picks stabbing into his ears. He squeezed his eyes shut and strained to keep the air in his lungs. The artificial gravity beneath him disengaged, the outer door opened, and a blast of air expelled him from the ship like garbage. He spun uncontrollably through the frigid void of space.

Jeremy thought his grand plan had failed. Hille should have already retrieved him. Maybe Davenport's lightning weapon had really destroyed her or damaged her memory again? In his panicked state, he uncontrollably exhaled.

***

Light began filtering through Jeremy's frozen eyelids, and he inhaled a breath of fresh air. He was freezing and couldn't move, but he was alive. When he tried to speak, he only mumbled.

"I can't understand a word you're saying," Hille said. "You need to an-nun-ci-ate." She overpronounced each syllable.

Jeremy felt a warm tingling sensation from Hille's medical treatment and knew she was repairing any cellular damage resulting from his impromptu spacewalk. Forcing his mouth to move properly, he dribbled out, "What took you so long?"

"Oh, I had to make it look convincing. If those goons had been looking out the airlock, they would have seen me swoop in and pick you up."

"I thought Davenport destroyed you," he said slowly—talking was becoming less a chore.

"Pfff." She flipped her hand. "That amateur won't destroy me, but I'll give you some kudos for anticipating his attack."

"You're the only thing that presents a threat to his plan, so I knew he would be prepared."

"Score one for the near-frozen human." She winked at him.

"I almost had the flagship ejected out the airlock."

"That was a crazy long shot, and it would have only delayed him at best."

"How far are we from the weapon?" he asked.

"Davenport's ship will rendezvous in seven minutes," she said.

"That's not long," Jeremy said. "How did we get there so fast?"

"Your little escapade took longer than expected, and they toted the *Summa Celestial* down to the engineering deck and rigged it to a super-duper power shunt. Now the ship goes much faster."

"Then he's cracked the virus," Jeremy said in a grim tone.

Hille scrunched up her face while she thought for a second. "I'm guessing here, but I bet he's only able to access rudimentary functionality. Power is obviously on that list, but if he had full access, he would just use the flagship to destroy Earth."

"Can we just ram the weapon and break it apart?" he asked. "We know it's made of engine rings produced by the Corporation and not some exotic alien alloy."

"Remember that zappy-lightning gun?" Hille asked. "Um-hum. Now, imagine it powered by a big old star instead of primitive Earth-made power cells. If I break my cloak for an instant, they'll fry me, and you, to a crisp."

"We can't let him destroy Earth," Jeremy said. "Get me back on the ship, and I'll do something. You can get Alice and go on to Mars or back to Earth if I'm successful."

"That's brave and all, but suicidal."

"The indentured crew will help me," Jeremy added. "The two I ran into said they were part of your resistance. There are probably more."

"It'll take time for the weapon to charge. You've got until then to pull a rabbit out of your hat."

"I've still got a camo suit. I can disguise myself as security and shut off the power."

Hille held up a palm to silence Jeremy. "Something's up over there."

Jeremy turned to look at the image displayed on the wall. A large panel on top of Davenport's ship retracted, and a parabolic dish, ten meters across, rose out of the opening. The structure was mounted on a telescoping tower and extended another twenty meters above the ship and rotated fifteen degrees port. After a few seconds of minor adjustments, a bluish-white line of light streaked out of it into space. The beam grew in diameter until it filled the diameter of the dish and became so bright it illuminated the enormous structure of joined rings a thousand kilometers away.

"He's transferring energy from the flagship to the weapon," Hille said. "I can already detect gravitational fluctuations."

"Show me a diagram on a scale of the Earth-Mars orbits," Jeremy said.

The display on the wall changed, and Jeremy studied the diagram. "He's deflecting Mars' gravity so it will push the Earth toward the Sun and cause a catastrophic event."

"The weapon will be at full power in twenty-three minutes and nineteen seconds," Hille said.

Jeremy thought about the direness of their situation. The fate of every living soul on Earth was at stake, but that wasn't his primary concern. It was Alice. The last year hadn't been the best for them, and it was his fault. He had lost himself in the task at hand, just like he had done with his senior project. He sacrificed everything then to become a full employee. And for what? All he did was put his friends in danger to build a stupid spaceship, something the Corporation wasn't interested in anyway. He thought he had learned from his mistakes, but he had done it again. His valiant crusade against the Corporation had already cost Ron's life, and Alice was Davenport's prisoner.

While torturing himself with past failures, something struck Jeremy. It was the birth of an idea. It was a way to make all the work he had done in the past pay off.

"Do you still have my engine rings we used to get back to Earth?" he asked.

Hille nodded. "They're in storage."

"Are they operational?" A glimmer appeared in Jeremy's eyes.

"I believe so." Her avatar wrinkled its forehead, displaying her confusion.

"I need a power supply and a field modulator that we can control remotely."

"How much power is required?"

"The same output as the power packs Ron made on the Moon."

"Done," she said, and the bottom of the sphere rippled as the stacked one-meter rings rose out of the floor. "I've installed the modulator and connected the power supply." She rubbed her hands together.

"When Davenport's ship passes by the weapon, we can drop my engine off ten-thousand kilometers into the field at this point." He pressed his finger on the diagram in the middle of the cone-shaped distortion field.

"It'll be a bumpy ride," she said. "Then we get Alice?"

"We have to save the indentured, too," Jeremy added. "For Ron."

"That's fifty-eight people," Hille said in a higher tone than usual. "As much as I would love to accommodate them, I'm not a bus."

"I have an idea," Jeremy said.

CHAPTER 15

THE CHARLIE MANEUVER

The gravitational disturbance projected by Davenport's weapon was jarring. Even Hille's advanced technology couldn't compensate for the immense power emanating from the structure, and it had only reached fifty percent of its output. At full power, the gravitational ripples would shift the orbit of a planet over fifty-five million kilometers away.

"We're in position," Hille said, unaffected by the turbulence. The same laws of physics affecting Jeremy did not apply to her avatar.

"Deploy. Deploy. Deploy," Jeremy said, struggling to speak through the jostling.

Hille changed the display on the sphere's wall to show an omnidirectional view of the surrounding space. There was a thump when she spit out Jeremy's senior project from inverted space. The two rings were stacked on top of one another, giving the appearance of a single, thicker ring. Hille had added the power pack and control module as an additional layer. The gravitational disturbance buffeted the free-floating object, causing it to spin wildly and move away on an erratic trajectory.

"I'm activating standby mode." He tapped a few commands into the input panel at the tip of his chair's armrest.

The engine rings immediately stopped gyrating and oriented to face the massive weapon. Hille and Jeremy chaotically bounced about while his lunar engine hung motionless in space.

"I don't want to rain on your parade," Hille said, "but those itty-bitty rings and that micro power supply won't even register on that ginormous death machine aimed at Earth."

"It'll work." He had spent a significant chunk of his life working on gravitational deflection. Hille's lack of confidence in his plan would have normally concerned him, but not this time. Davenport had co-opted his near-body engine project to further his own goals, so Jeremy's deflection method wasn't part of the aliens' field-theory lexicon. That meant it had a chance.

"Now what?" she asked, hand on hip.

Jeremy paused for a second. "I need you to phase through Davenport's ship and drop me off by Alice's cell."

"And then?"

"Hide inside the ship somewhere."

"And then?" Hille emphasized the last word this time.

"We somehow convince Davenport to go into Alice's quarters and blast him with the virus signal he was using on her."

Hille paused while she considered Jeremy's proposition. "That might work," she finally said, "but how will you lure him into the trap?"

"I'll offer him something he can't resist."

***

After a rough, ten-minute ride out of the gravitational wake, Hille and Jeremy emerged right on the tail of Davenport's ship.

"Why can't Davenport detect your cloak?" Jeremy asked.

"I seem to have knowledge of key Syndicate technologies, and they're the best at subterfuge. Their cloaking technology is the only reason they've existed this long in the Intergalactic Corp's universe."

"Are they the same...species?"

"We're all techno-beings," she said. "The differences are more in line with who got which software patch and which databases grant you access."

"What other Syndicate technology would Davenport be unaware of?"

"The Syndicate likes to co-opt people just like the operative took over the real Theodor Davenport. The Intergalactic Corp usually creates a simulacrum, an android-like construct, to impersonate other life forms."

"I bet he was leaving evidence to point at the Syndicate in case he got caught."

"Possibly," she said. "The Intergalactic Corp's M.O. is generally centered around predicting the future and making minor adjustments to affect the outcome, whereas the Syndicate uses brute-force and would never have waited a hundred years to carry out a plan."

"Davenport is from the Intergalactic Corp, but he acts like he's from the Syndicate. He has also lived as a human longer than most humans," Jeremy said. "It'll be impossible to guess what he might do."

"I'm not the one you want to ask, but he is a diehard supporter of the Intergalactic Corp. He will likely stay true to his origin. However, he doesn't always follow the predicted path."

Jeremy rolled his eyes. "Thanks. You're not very helpful."

"I told you to come up with a plan on your own so he won't anticipate it. You spent a year hiding out in a Syndicate moon base with one of their AIs. Use that experience to your advantage."

Jeremy shook his head. "The fate of the world shouldn't be resting on my shoulders."

"That may very well be the reason we kick Davenport's ass," Hille said. "Oh, and the Earth-destroying death weapon is up to seventy percent output."

"Show me where Alice is."

The wall display changed to a schematic view of Davenport's ship. A blue dot pulsed at Alice's location, and dozens of green dots showed the indentured crew. Twelve red points showed the security detail, and a gold circle located Davenport on the ship's bridge.

"How fast can you make me one of those android impersonators?"

A ball small enough to fit in Jeremy's hand popped out of the wall and rolled toward his chair.

"That fast," she said.

"It doesn't look like an android to me."

"Tap it three times with your index finger to activate." Hille's avatar motioned the action in the air.

"How do I select the identity?"

"I've updated your display card to let you select."

"I'll need more of these," Jeremy said, holding up the ball.

***

"Prepare for drop-off," Hille said, voice only. She had reduced her diameter to the smallest size that could still accommodate her passenger.

Jeremy crouched, wearing a camouflage suit of Ron's design, all black and covered with white disks. He held a simulacrum ball in one hand and a small bag in the other.

"Here we go." The exotic fields she projected around her hull warped the physical matter of Davenport's ship around her sphere.

Three security guards stood outside Alice's cell. They didn't see Hille approaching, just a blob of distortion. An arc of electricity shot out and dropped the three men to the floor.

Alice jumped up and pressed her face against the cold glass door. The guards were gone, and Jeremy stood outside her makeshift cell.

"Come with me." He unlatched the door, tapped the simulacrum ball three times, and threw it into her cell. Copper-colored filaments sprouted out of the orb and wove themselves into a mesh approximating a human figure. It flickered a few times and a holographic shell that looked exactly like Alice manifested. It took a seat on the floor where she had been and paid no attention to Jeremy or the real Alice.

"I thought you were dead again," she said. "How did you get free?"

"Hille," he said. "We've got to get to your quarters." He tapped his display card, and his camo suit changed his appearance to mimic the shortest of the incapacitated security guards.

On the way to Alice's quarters, another security guard approached them.

"Just look straight ahead," Jeremy whispered. "Don't pay any attention to him." He tried to raise himself up on his toes, but even then, he was only the same height as Alice.

The guard turned to look at them when they passed. Jeremy knew something registered, but he didn't take any action.

"That was close," Alice said as soon as they were out of earshot.

Then they heard running footsteps behind them.

"He's coming back. We've got to hide." Jeremy used his spanner on the nearest door, and they slipped inside a supply closet.

Three minutes later, after the corridor was clear, they reached Alice's quarters. The door hissed open before Jeremy could even reach for his spanner.

"I was expecting you." Davenport stood in the middle of Alice's quarters with a toothy smile on his face.

Alice jumped.

Jeremy eyed the CEO, showing no hint of fear. "I'm here to stop you from destroying Earth."

Security personnel approached from both directions of the corridor, forcing Jeremy and Alice inside the cabin.

Davenport walked around his captives to stand next to the security detail. He was a tall man, well over two meters, but his height started to shrink, and his appearance morphed into something more feminine.

The guards reacted with confusion as the simulacrum took on Hille's appearance. She then grabbed all four of the security team at once and released a jolt of electricity, knocking them unconscious.

"We're not done yet." Jeremy went over to a wall panel and pressed an intercom button. "Davenport, I have something you want."

Someone would need to relay the message to the CEO, giving Jeremy time to override the controls on the room's signal emitters. Hille had already loaded a program to do the work; he just had to run it.

"For a failed trainee, you are very difficult to get rid of," Davenport's voice said over the speaker in the ceiling.

"I'm here to make a deal," Jeremy said.

"I cannot imagine anything you could have that would interest me," Davenport said.

"I have the key to unlock the virus," Jeremy said. "It can free all the alien technology. All of it, not just its basic functionality."

There was an audible snort over the speaker.

"Hildegard had the antidote inside of her, and I've downloaded it to my display card." Jeremy held up the small rectangle between his thumb and forefinger. He was sure cameras were watching him.

"And how did a primitive like you uncover that?" Davenport's skepticism emanated through the com.

"It was how she infected the AI running the moon base. Just making a connection shut the entire base down. It didn't make sense that she would be immune and transmit the virus to other aliens. I also noticed that the signal you were blasting Alice with was identical to Hille's standard communication handshake."

Davenport didn't respond.

"The antidote is simple. You just need the key to turn off the virus," Jeremy bluffed. "Let Alice and me go, don't destroy Earth, and you can have a fully functional alien flagship. Go plunder the universe, I don't care, but you have to leave this solar system alone."

The door to the corridor hissed open, and Davenport strutted in, followed by several of his men. He held a rod in his hand that Jeremy thought was one of the electrocution sticks his bodyguard had used before to kill Eric, but this one was different. He leveled it toward Jeremy, and a beam of energy shot out of its end. Hille's simulacrum lurched in front of the blast, and the android body was reduced to a charred mess of bent wire.

Jeremy pressed a button on his display card to activate the room's signal emitters.

"That will not work," Davenport said. "I dispatched all virus-related technology when I had the *Summa Celestial's* power supply unlocked. It was too dangerous to keep around."

Jeremy's readouts showed the virus-laden signal was flooding the room at full strength, but a closer look revealed the power consumption and ambient signal strength were negligible.

Davenport's smirk grew larger than Jeremy had ever seen it.

"I may not be able to infect you, but I can destroy your weapon." He used his display card to signal the package Hille dropped off in the gravitational distortion.

"My weapon is almost at full capacity. You cannot stop it now."

Jeremy shook his head. "I needed you to get the power output close to a hundred percent." His tone was confident, considering the perilous situation he was in. "You realize that this is my field of expertise. I may not be some alien supercomputer, but I came up with the method you're using to destroy the Earth. You just stole the concept, and you never considered its weaknesses. You should have done the research."

"I'm tired of this." Davenport turned to his security team. "Kill them."

The security guards moved toward Jeremy and Alice.

"You're too late," Jeremy said.

A flash outside the cabin's window preceded an alarm over the ship's speakers.

The security personnel stopped and looked back at Davenport for instructions.

"There's a chain reaction cascading through that network of rings. I took out the center section allowing a feedback loop to overload the remaining nodes," Jeremy said.

"That's impossible," Davenport said.

"I reflected some of the gravitational distortions you were focusing on Earth back at the weapon. That's what my near-body propulsion engine did. All I needed to do was push a few pieces of the structure out of place. This technique of multi-directional deflection was in my project reports."

Davenport flicked through several pages of information on his display card. His face drooped as a scowl formed. "You have only delayed my plans." He stared at the guards. "Finish them."

Two of the guards plunged their electrocution sticks into Jeremy and Alice's chests and released an arc of electricity into their bodies.

Davenport smiled at having eliminated the source of his problems, but then he noticed that both figures still stood and blinked to reveal a copper-colored wire mesh. "Find them!"

The security men ran out of the cabin, leaving Davenport alone in the room.

The CEO didn't notice the distorted circle forming in the ceiling above him. It rippled as it grew until a transparent sphere dropped, capturing Davenport inside. Hille had shrunk to a two-meter diameter, forcing Davenport to stoop inside his new prison. He repeatedly fired his weapon, but to no effect.

"That won't work." Her voice boomed inside the sphere. "Now, it's my turn." She flooded her interior with the virus signal. Jeremy wasn't lying about her handshake being the same as the virus signal Davenport used on Alice.

Davenport grabbed his head, trying to block the signal, but there was nothing he could do. He fell to the floor unconscious.

The real Jeremy and Alice entered the room. They had been controlling the simulacrums remotely.

"It's done," Hille said.

"We watched," he said. "Nice job. If we ever get Charlie running again, we'll have to thank him for that trick."

"What just happened?" Alice asked.

"We had to get Davenport alone," Jeremy said. "To do this." He pulled another copper-colored ball out of his pocket, tapped it three times, and dropped it onto the floor.

The ball sprouted filaments and quickly wove itself into a tall figure. It flickered and appeared to look just like Davenport.

"This is the only way to get the indentured safely to Mars."

CHAPTER 16

THE MARS COLONY

ONE YEAR LATER ON MARS. The Earth was safe, yet a few dozen kilometers closer to the Sun. Davenport's weapon would have required several days to accumulate enough change in the orbit to create a catastrophic event. Beyond a few minor earthquakes and unusual weather phenomena, the people of Earth were unaware of their near disaster.

Davenport's expedition to Mars reached operational status more quickly than planned. Instead of using domes on the surface, its premise had been to use old lava tubes as the foundation for speedy underground construction on the red planet. Each shipment of components for the gravity weapon also brought supplies and prefab modules for colony construction. Davenport planned to live there, presumably forever, after destroying Earth and wanted to be well-equipped.

The colonization plan also called for the use of fifty-thousand indentured employees to assemble three new bases connected by tube trains. They were to move the modules into the tunnel systems and seal off the Martian landscape. These were dangerous jobs for what Davenport viewed as a crew of expendable cogs. Hille modified this part of his plan by producing an army of simulacrum workers to carry out all the construction tasks. These workers never tired; needed no air, food, or water; and were genuinely expendable. She also controlled each one, eliminating ethical questions of a new slave race to replace the previous one. The android workers brought a well-developed colony to life in record time with a fresh population awaiting their first taste of freedom.

If the alien-controlled Davenport could fake a Mars colony for over a decade, Hille could fake a CEO until they restructured the Corporation to no longer require him. Nobody even noticed it wasn't the same Davenport at the Corporation's helm other than he had gotten a lot nicer to his employees. The real Theodor Davenport VI was alive but unconscious. He had been under alien control for at least forty years. Hille believed he would recover someday, but his problems were beyond her medical capabilities. The sleeping techno-being was still inside his head and could be a potential threat if the virus ever lost its grip.

Alice sprang her parents from the corporate retraining center with a memo from the new Hille-controlled Davenport. She had them put on the next transport to Mars, and they arrived four months later. They worked alongside the formerly indentured, finishing out the colony, and were happy to leave the stressful life of the Corporation behind.

Hille suggested they hide the *Summa Celestial* in a secret location on Mars. Jeremy and Alice agreed that the flagship was too dangerous for anyone else to know about. The alien-controlled Davenport had unlocked enough of the its functionality to power his weapon, and the full effect of that change was unknown. Hille monitored it with great attention but had detected no increased activity.

"So, what do we do now?" Jeremy asked.

"You're running this show," Hille said. "I'm just doing all the work." She now used a simulacrum body to interact with other people. It didn't have the limitations of the holographic projection, and it allowed her to be in multiple places at the same time with different identities.

"We continue to help Earth," Alice said. "Free the rest of the indentured from their slavery to the Corporation. Humankind shouldn't be controlled by a handful of elites, alien or not, and the Corporation isn't the only hegemon on Earth."

"That's going to take time," Jeremy said. "If we free all the indentured at once, the Corporation will collapse, and we need to keep it strong enough to foil the competitors Davenport didn't control." He paused. "And we need to be prepared for the possibility of more alien intervention."

"Nobody said that making the Earth a better place would be easy," Alice said. "And the policy changes we've put in place have already made life better for the employees, especially the indentured."

"And what about Mars?" Jeremy asked. "We've implemented Davenport's colonization plan. Should we continue developing it?"

"I ran the numbers," Alice said. "We can't continue without additional resources. Davenport had sent a lot of supplies from Earth, and we won't have that stockpile for future expansion."

"You two need to start thinking outside the box," Hille said. "You have connections." She pointed to herself with both hands.

"I know you can fabricate a lot, but can you make enough to build a new city?" Jeremy asked.

"I can with a solar-system-sized power source buried in the backyard."

"And you're not worried about waking it up?" Alice asked.

"I've been poking around to make sure that the *Summa Celestial* is dormant, and I found something."

"Is the virus breaking down?" Jeremy asked, the alarm evident in his voice.

"No. No." She waved her hands. "Nothing so dramatic."

Jeremy cocked his head, waiting for her to elaborate.

"I think I found Skylar Holden inside the flagship."

"He would be at least a hundred and eighty years old, wouldn't he?" Alice asked.

"He and his wife, Victoria, are trapped inside a shrinking inverted gravity bubble. Time has essentially stopped for them. If we can get them out…"

"They could answer a lot of questions," Jeremy said. "And we would have someone with experience dealing with aliens."

Hille made an exaggerated nod.

Jeremy's display card chimed. "We've got to go."

Hille squinted. "Where?"

"There's a new bar in the promenade that serves food packets. I'm finally paying my debt to Alice by taking her out to dinner."

Alice nodded.

"Hmm," Hille snorted. "A couple of years late."

"In my defense, we spent most of that time hiding from the Corporation. We also saved Earth and built a Mars colony."

Hille paused for a split second as she queried the base's information. "I see you named the place 'Ron's'."

Jeremy nodded.

"Nice," she said. "I think he would approve."

"Do you want to come with us?" Jeremy said, straining not to sound dissuading.

"Heavens, no. I've got some super-duper meditation to catch up on." She smiled.

"Okay," Jeremy said, and he and Alice left holding hands.

ABOUT THE AUTHOR

Joey Rogers is an enthusiast of sci-fi, video games, and all-around geekery. He's a software developer by day in the high-tech city of Huntsville, Alabama and loves writing about what the future might hold. His other novels are:

THE BELFORE VOID

A FUNNY THING HAPPENED ON THE MOON

AN ALIEN, A TIME MACHINE, AND A LOSER

AN ALIEN, A TIME MACHINE, AND A HERO

Website: www.gegodyne.com

Twitter: @gegodyne

Email: gegodyne@gmail.com

Facebook: www.facebook.com/gegodyne